P9-CDU-595

TINY CRIMES

TINY CRIMES

VERY SHORT TALES OF MYSTERY AND MURDER

EDITED BY LINCOLN MICHEL & NADXIELI NIETO

This is a work of fiction. All of the characters, organizations, and events portrayed in this anthology either are products of the authors' imaginations or are used fictitiously.

Anthology selection copyright © 2018 by Lincoln Michel and Nadxieli Nieto.
Interior illustrations copyright © 2018 by Wesley Allsbrook. Printed by permission of the artist.
First published in the United States in 2018 by Black Balloon, an imprint of Catapult (catapult.co).
All rights reserved.

Cover and book design by Nadxieli Nieto
Interior illustrations by Wesley Allsbrook

ISBN: 978-1-936787-87-6

Catapult titles are distributed to the trade by Publishers Group West.
Phone: 866-400-5351

Library of Congress Control Number: 2017954702

Printed in Canada

10 9 8 7 6 5 4 3 2 1

TO EVERYONE WHO HELPED US BURY THE BODIES.
WE'LL NEVER RAT YOU OUT.

CONTENTS

INTRODUCTION

LINCOLN MICHEL AND NADXIELI NIETO

The great Samuel Delany once said, "The only important elements in any society are the artistic and the criminal, because they alone, by questioning the society's values, can force it to change." When artists turn their attention to the criminal, their work becomes that much more powerful. In *Tiny Crimes*, we've asked some of our favorite writers to examine the current state of the criminal, the illegal, and the depraved. These are stories of gigantic crimes—vicious murders, insider robberies, white-collar criminals with blood on their hands—but each is short enough to be read during a coffee break or a corporate break-in.

Crime is the borderland of culture, but a border that is forever changing. What is illegal or unacceptable one day may become the status quo the next. Do-gooders are thrown in jail. Criminals are elected. Crime fiction, writ small or large, helps map our cultural consciousness: Who do we now think are the criminals? Gangsters? Politicians? Police? All of us?

The stories in *Tiny Crimes* trace tales of loneliness and betrayal, cataloging our desire for love, money, and revenge; the estranging solitude of a new city; the drug-fueled afternoon that gets out of hand; the fear for and of children, as well as of doctors, sex-positive women (yes, still!), the government; and experiments scientific, social, and rhetorical gone awry. Here too we find the old fears (and aspirations)—the glinting knives and secret signals of the furtive class. But double-crossers and murderous femmes fatales aren't always the bad guys. Sometimes we're rooting for them as they narrowly get out alive or bake their revenge into human empanadas. The joy is not as much in the *whodunit* as in the *who got it good*.

The crimes collected here take place not only among the alleys of rain-streaked metropolises but also in the backyards of gated communities, in swamplands, doctors' offices, and suburban malls. They take place over email and voicemail, in whispered exchanges, and on social media. In one story we are the unrepentant victor, in the next the victim, in others we are merely the people who clean up the mess. Crime fiction, and noir in particular, has always blurred the line between

x

criminal and good guy, arguing that rarely are the two mutually exclusive. And even the most glancing look at the daily news reveals that reality is no different, and no less strange.

We hope you enjoy.

Sincerely,
Lincoln Michel and Nadxieli Nieto

TINY CRIMES

CIRCUIT CITY

J. ROBERT LENNON

Because we didn't like John, our manager, and because we suspected that he planned to rob Circuit City on its final day of operations, we decided (John, John, and I) to rob Circuit City on its final day of operations.

John had been tasked with selling off all stock, which meant deep discounts for our customers on computers, televisions, stereo equipment, video games, DVDs, and home appliances. John elected to close Circuit City for one week leading up to its final day of operations, which was Sunday, March 8, 2009, in order to generate excitement and to promote the store clearance as a "sales event." The "sales event" would be cash-only, which is an unorthodox procedure at

Circuit City and which tipped John, John, and myself off to the possibility that John was planning to rob Circuit City. In movies and on television, which John, John, and I often were able to watch during our shifts at Circuit City, owing to its recent decline in revenue, this is known as a "heist."

"Cash," John observed, smoking, during our smoke break out on the loading dock, "is harder to account for than other forms of payment."

"John is going to steal some or all of the cash," John replied, smoking.

Smoking, I said, "If John intends to steal some or all of the cash, then we should steal some or all of the cash instead." In movies and on television, this is known as a "double cross."

We all were wearing the red shirts required of all employees. John wore the required red shirt as well, but upon his required shirt was embroidered the word "Manager." Because we didn't like John, we called him Manager.

"Manager, this customer is looking for a game controller."

"Manager, this customer would like to return these cables."

"Manager, your required red shirt is looking fly today."

"Stop calling me that."

"Stop calling me that."

"Stop calling me that."

The "sales event" proved successful. Customers lined up around the building in order to buy computers, televisions, stereo equipment, video games, DVDs, and home appliances, all the way back to the loading dock where no one was smoking due to the "sales event." Circuit City made $42,738 in the hours until noon, at which time John reduced prices by half, then Circuit City made another $29,722 in the hours until five p.m., at which time John reduced prices to 90 percent off list, then Circuit City made another $22,835 in the hours until closing, for a grand total of $95,295, which we helped John pack into large canvas sacks. In movies and on television, this is known as "loot."

John, John, and I made to leave Circuit City, driving in John's car, after farewells and thank-yous to John, whom we didn't call Manager for the first time ever. John appeared moved but eager for us to leave, presumably because John was also eager to transfer the large canvas sacks of dollars into his car. We came back five minutes later to find John at the loading bay, loading the large canvas sacks of dollars into his car.

"Manager, what are you doing?"

"Manager, are those the dollars?"

"Manager, this is an unorthodox procedure."

"Hey, well now," John said, and then John pulled a pistol from the crack of his ass and shot John in the head. John collapsed to the ground beside his blood-spattered car, his red shirt, bearing the embroidered word "Manager," soaked red with blood, which was ironic. The shooting was an unorthodox procedure. In movies and on television, this is known as a "twist." After a moment of reflection, John and I began to transfer the large canvas sacks of dollars from John's car to John's car. John asked John if he intended to help, and John replied, gesturing toward John's lifeless body, "I just did. Also," he said, smoking, which was an orthodox procedure, especially considering that John, John, and I were at the loading dock and were now on what could be termed a permanent smoke break, "it's my car. John," he said, meaning me, "you drive," and he gestured toward the driver's-side door. I got into the car, behind the steering wheel. Driving John's car was an unorthodox procedure. Outside the car, John shot John in much the way he had shot John. Now I understood that John was bad. In the movies and on television, this is known as "anagnorisis." The cigarette fell out of John's mouth, and he said fuck.

John climbed into the passenger seat and pointed his pistol at me and said drive. I drove. John said left. John said left. John said right. John said keep going. John said shut up. John said keep going. John said exit. John said right. John said, his voice distorted by the rutted dirt road we were driving on, keep going.

Now John's portable telephone rang. In movies and on television this is known as "deus ex machina." John looked down. I reached behind my back and pulled out the pistol I'd hidden in the crack of my ass and I pointed it at John. In movies and on television, this is known as "peripeteia." I told John to drop his pistol and instead John pointed his pistol at me, so I shot John, and he shot me. We shot each other. In movies and on television, this is known as "poetic justice." We died.

We kept driving. This was an unorthodox procedure. Our red shirts were red. The dirt road smoothed out and began to glow. Angels appeared on either side of the car to escort us into heaven. In movies and on television, I am known as an "unreliable narrator." Circuit City was later purchased by Systemax and consolidated, along with CompUSA, into the TigerDirect online brand. This is an orthodox procedure. John and I are still driving. The angels wear red. John and I are beginning to think that they are not angels and that this is not heaven.

ANY OTHER

JAC JEMC

He found her already seated at the coffee shop.

"It's so nice to finally meet you." He held out his hand.

Bethany paused before accepting.

"I'm Keith," he said once her fingers were wrapped in his, and laughed at himself. "Of course, you know that. I'm sorry. May I?" He gestured to the chair across from her.

Bethany nodded, wondered why he didn't get himself a cup of coffee first.

"No use in wasting time, so I'll just ask," he said. "Have you made a decision?"

Bethany responded honestly. She shook her head.

"Good, then I can still convince you." Keith

scooted his chair forward. "I know it's a family heirloom, but if you keep it locked away in storage, what difference does it make if you technically own it or someone else does? If you sell it to me, you can visit it. I can loan it to you. We could even agree that you can buy it back at any time."

Bethany wondered why it mattered so much to him. That he wanted it so very badly made her want to refuse him the satisfaction. "How much are you willing to pay?" she asked.

Keith blinked rapidly. "Well, we discussed fifty thousand dollars."

Bethany frowned. She had learned to do this during negotiations of any kind.

Keith filled his lungs. "But I'm prepared to go up to seventy-five thousand dollars." He looked down at her coffee cup now, ready to wait for her response.

"Would you get me a refill?" she asked. She enjoyed this power. She held it tight.

Keith jumped up. "Of course!" She could feel his relief at stepping away from her decision-making. He ushered her mug over to the counter and asked the barista for a cup of his own, as well. She watched him closely as he pulled out a few bills. She examined the repetitive wear of his wallet on his back pocket. She noticed the bevel of the outside heels of his shoes, the evidence of uncorrected supination and thriftiness. The money he offered her could be better spent.

When Keith returned, he looked expectant, hopeful the delay might have delivered a verdict.

He sipped his coffee. "I'm happy to answer any questions." He smiled.

Bethany found the way he forced himself to keep his gaze on her willful. She respected his determination and broke eye contact to see his index finger fidget the cuticle of his thumb, torn raw and red.

"Or maybe I can ask you a question," Keith said. "What's holding you back? Why not sell it?" He lifted his mug to his lips again.

Something about this query settled it for Bethany. "I'm sorry," she said. "No deal."

Keith set his mug down a little too hard. Coffee rushed over the edge of the cup and ran down the tilt of the table into his lap. "Shoot," he said. He ran to retrieve some napkins, wiping first at the splash on his pants and then mopping at the edges of the mug on the table. Bethany didn't move or speak. When Keith finally resettled, he said, "Why?"

Bethany looked in Keith's eyes for the answer, but all she turned up was the realization that she didn't need to explain it to him. She felt her shoulders flinch, as if the decision mattered little to her, no possibility of reversing it.

"There's nothing I can do to convince you?"

She shook her head and tightened her lips.

Keith stood, a ball of wet napkins clenched in his fist. "Okay," he said. "You know where to find me if you change your mind." Blood swamped her heart. "Have a good afternoon then," Keith said. He turned away, but spun back again. "I don't have it, but if I'd offered a hundred thousand dollars, would that have made a difference?" he asked.

"No," she said. She held out her hand hoping to end the conversation as it had begun, before she remembered the wad of napkins. She placed her palm back on the table.

"Then why . . . all right. Thank you, Joanne." Adrenaline rushed behind the name "Joanne," but Bethany maintained her composure. Keith walked away with purpose. He pulled open the door and Bethany watched through the window as he disappeared right and then crossed back left, unfamiliar with the neighborhood or changing his mind about where he was headed.

Bethany wondered what it was Keith had wanted. She wondered what Joanne had to give. She wondered why she felt like it was her place to decide for both of them, but it had all unfolded so easily. She took a last sip of her coffee and gathered her things.

A woman in a polished pantsuit walked through the door, her eyes looking for someone. She asked at the counter about the man whom she was supposed to meet.

Bethany let her fingers fall on the shoulder of the woman as lightly as possible and leaned in. "Joanne?" The woman's whole body pursed under Bethany's touch. "Keep it," she whispered.

NOBODY CHECKS THEIR VOICEMAILS ANYMORE NOT EVEN DETECTIVES

SASHA FLETCHER

MONDAY, 9:12 A.M., 00:52

Jimmy, it's your girl. The one at the desk whom you pay a living wage. This is what could be known as a wake-up call if we were the sort of people who relied upon others to remind us of our tasks. I am aware this is funny seeing as my job partly entails me reminding you of various things and, to a certain extent, scheduling your life for you. The thing about that is that yesterday, Jim, note the shift to the more formal "Jim" here, it's meant to indicate a certain disdain here, *Jim*, yesterday you alerted me that you would be *looking into* an *incident* involving *a certain woman* who I *refuse to name*, due to the fact that she has not, as yet, bothered to pay for the one thousand billable hours on file. Life isn't free, Jim, and neither are the services of this office! Plus she tried to murder you fifteen times. Not that I'm counting. Anyway. The ghosts say hi. You know which ones.

MONDAY, 9 P.M., 00:03

Jim, you saved my life once and now you're responsible for it.

TUESDAY, 1:23 A.M., 00:02

Jim, I got that backward I'm sorry.

TUESDAY, 3:03 P.M., 00:58

Jim, I had a date yesterday. I can't tell if it went well. I can't tell much sometimes these days. You know that feeling, the one wherein the world is just not a thing you can find to be navigable? And how, *by the world*, I mean everything outside of you? The ways in which other people, in which other things, in which all others in toto, are not and will never be you? Or of a part with you? In your more romantic moments, Jim, you'd assure me that this was fine. That we're all flailing about blindly in the darkness, looking for a light switch, or a human connection. Just some signal in the dark. You'd tell me, Jim, that, well . . . Jim I'm sorry. I'm a bit high right now. In the office. It's essentially three o'clock on a Tuesday. One woman was in about a diamond. It turned out to be where you'd expect. A husband came in, for reasons unknown, with a check that cleared, and in a fashion I'd call timely. We're out of coffee. Don't worry though. Outside the door of the room I'm in it says, *We're on the case.* So. It's handled.

THURSDAY, 1:45 P.M., 00:46

Jimmy, come home, it's Thursday. Yesterday the fellow with the buffalo chicken wraps was downstairs. I got one for you, but then I ate it, because we both know they have to be eaten fresh. I saw that man I told you about again. It was as though a light shone down upon us from beyond. I held his hands in mine and asked him if he'd fuck me in the bathroom. He did. You can't trust a man who wouldn't do a thing like that if you asked him, Jim. I will either burn him in effigy or have dinner with him, later, tonight. If he tries a single thing without my asking, I will put one in his kneecap. When you hear this, if you do not smile in appreciation, then I hope you never come back, Jim. I hope you stay wherever the fuck you are. There is a pile of clues here just waiting for you if you'd only bother to look for them. I swear to God.

15

SUNDAY, 12:10 P.M., 00:32

Jim, it's Sunday. I made that man stake out your apartment with me. I wore a wig. I gave him a fake mustache, and I intend to make him keep it. Jim, you haven't been home, or to work. I know this because I have got my ways. It's why you hired me. I burned sage around your door. I feel like there're some fucked-to-death ghosts in your life, Jim. But I feel like you're maybe okay with this. I feel like maybe letting them eat your heart out is what you need. I feel like for some reason you're the kind of person who could need a thing like that. Why in the world that could be, I would not say.

SUNDAY, 11:50 P.M., 00:53

Jim, when I was a girl, were I ever a girl, I went by Rebecca. I was the kind of girl a boy'd swim across a lake and run through a meadow at dusk for, a boy who'd break curfew just to smell the kind of promise a girl like me contained. I was, those summers, a promise. I was made of the kind of stuff you beat your heart off to. I dreamed of a boy, the kind who'd swim across a lake and emerge, his curls dripping with water soon to dry in the sun before it fades, running through a meadow, needing me like air. I called him Bob, in my heart. Bob and Becca I carved, gently, somewhere I never thought anyone'd see, and they never did. Jim, we've all known what it's like to imagine longing, but that doesn't prepare us for longing. Our imaginations are fucked machines, Jim. And it's beautiful. Today there was a woman, and she wept. I could not say why, as she did not herself tell me. More tomorrow, as that's what it's there for.

TUESDAY, 10:10 A.M., 00:26

What in the hell, Jim. Three women have lost their husbands and would like you to find them. One young boy is wondering about his father. A fortune, untold, waits, obscured, by uncountable troubles. The police have shot four people today for, as far as I can tell, breathing. I have taken it upon us to investigate. The office took a vote this morning. It was me and the ghosts in favor, and the opposition has yet to return our calls. That's the news from here, Jimmy boy. All else forthcoming.

GIVE ME STRENGTH

KAREN HEULER

I first saw the patient Julie B. about a year ago, after her tests came in. She behaved as all newly diagnosed patients do—a blurt, a start, some protests of error. She felt fine; she felt well; I must be mistaken.

I'm an expert on the disease, you see. I like it because it has the most interesting range of side effects. It can manifest itself in contradictory signs and symptoms, some of them metaphorical, some of them physical. Seeing a new patient is like opening a new book.

"What did you say it was?" my new patient asked.

"It's commonly known as Writer's Scourge."

"I'm a writer."

I nodded. "My patients usually are."

She shuddered. "What will happen to me?"

"What kind of writing do you do?"

"Mysteries. I write mysteries. Cozies, you know; sort of pastoral."

Ah, good, I thought; I'd already had locked-door writers and police procedurals. The first one, by the way, went through a period of misapplying punctuation; for a while he lost all semicolons. I gave him a round of my experimental drug and he got them back. I gave him a placebo and he lost them again.

A lot of them have minor symptoms, you see; they have trouble with printing or they can't think up titles; but some of the really bad ones lose their endings. They just stop somewhere in a book or story and that's it. It's no use trying to coax them through it; they no longer understand what endings are all about. I had dinner with one of them just last month; he drinks a lot now because he feels uneasy but can't really say why. I kept trying to provoke his memory, saying things like, "And I remember a book you wrote where it was a knife of ice that was used as the weapon, do you remember that?" He got a faraway look. "Ice," he said. "I don't get it." Sad, really; he was writing books with crimes he couldn't solve.

Mostly they don't even know what their deficit is. Once it sets in fully, you see, they can't understand that anything has changed. "All I do is write," they say, "and no one will publish me! I don't understand it! I used to be big!"

I tell them they'll be big again. I lie. I tell them anything I like. Some of them I give my special medicine to; some of them I don't. I am interested in the development of disease, especially diseases that can twist and turn like a soap opera. At the last minute, if I choose, I can give them my medicine, which I call Strength, you see, because it lifts them up again. They sit up straight and write again, as if nothing had ever gone wrong.

Oh yes, of course, my patient Julie B.

"What are you working on?" I asked.

"A woman's throat is slit in a bed-and-breakfast that used to be a country home. It is slit by a long thin piece of paper, though everyone thinks it's a razor. I thought it was very clever: murder by paper cut."

I looked at her fingers, which had thin angry cuts on them. It had already started.

A lot of times the disease itself is an homage to someone the patients admire—say, they begin to gamble or get seizures because they adore Dostoyevsky. Or they might move to Russia; many writers just move somewhere and we never know why. They make typos and move to Romania instead of Rome, Miami instead of Milan.

But that wasn't Julie B. I mentioned my cure. Experimental, I said; still in early tests, not for anyone at her stage.

She sucked on a paper cut. "What's going to happen to me?" she finally groaned, clutching her head.

"I'd like you to keep a record," I said with a great

21

deal of encouragement. "Keep a list of things you can remember each day—good titles, enticing phrases, character names, possible plots. Write them down each day. The list will keep getting shorter, but it won't bother you. That's a blessing, isn't it?"

"I don't feel blessed," she grumped.

I gave her an appointment once a week.

When she came I went over her list, which she worked on dutifully. It was always neatly typed and proofread. She started with paragraphs, then sentences, then items such as:

> *Are any insects poisonous?*
> *John is the name of the hero.*
> *Avoid sentence fragments.*
> *Corpses are dead.*

She became increasingly haunted; her shoulders were bowed and sometimes she almost panted in fright. "Give me Strength," she said. "I feel so weak."

I shook my head internally. She wasn't bad enough, if she remembered that.

Finally one day she came in with:

> *Main character is evil.*
> *Murder everywhere.*
> *Chapters have a space at the top.*
> *Someone is after me.*

I placed that list on top of the others. I was sure it would be the last.

After that, things went downhill rapidly. She began to wear shawls and got a persecuted look. "Something is about to happen," she whispered, rolling her eyes, keeping her back to the wall. Less than a year and she'd come to this! She stood in the doorway, moving her body in agitation while her feet remained planted. She was very thin, and wrapped a scarf around her neck.

"He crept behind me and pulled my head back," she said hoarsely. "And then he cut from ear to ear."

I had to sigh with pleasure. She was driven mad with premonition some days; on others she was fatally absorbed by what had happened to her. She was no longer a writer, I could see. She had become one of her own characters; she was living as the character she would have written would have lived. And died, of course.

I became enamored of her flitting eyes, the tremor in her voice, the gentle pulse upon her neck. I could have given her Strength, but I never did. I never did.

EL LÚSER

YURI HERRERA

La mesa del feo malora brincó al ser golpeada por el portafolios del modesto catrín. La limonada sobre la mesa pegó a su vez un brinco milimétrico, se desplomó y el líquido se vertió sobre las rodillas de aquél. Modesto catrín era pesado pero como enclenque, y parecía de temperamento nervioso. Feo malora era calvo y orejón, más alto y más pesado que el otro, pero como fornido. Se levantó de su silla a velocidad media, lo que hizo pensar que estaba sosiego, sin embargo un segundo después le dio una pequeña bofetada a modesto catrín, sin mucha fuerza pero sonora.

—¿Qué te pasa, pendejito? ¿qué-te-pasa-qué-te-PÁ-sa?

THE LUSER

YURI HERRERA

TRANSLATED BY LISA DILLMAN

The ugly thug's table jolted when struck by the diffident spiff's briefcase. The lemonade on the table, in turn, gave its own miniature jolt, toppling, and liquid poured onto the former's knees. Diffident spiff was stocky but kind of wimpy, and seemed the nervous type. Ugly thug was bald and big eared, taller and stockier, but kind of brawny. He rose from his chair at average speed, which made it seem he was unperturbed, yet a second later gave diffident spiff a little slap—not too hard but loud.

"What's your problem, you little prick? What's-your-problem-what's-your-*prob*-lem?"

Acercó su frente a la de modesto catrín, sin llegar a tocarla, y desde su lado izquierdo disparó una bofetada con la mano entera. Modesto catrín trastabilló sobre su lado izquierdo y debió agarrarse de una silla para no caer.

Hasta ahí, la escena era emocionante y apenas incómoda, en todo caso asunto de alguien más. Pero feo malora soltó otra bofetada, artera, de arriba abajo, de esas mitad mejilla-mitad oreja que arden y aturden, y modesto catrín cayó al suelo.

—Ahora, así te me vas a la cocina, les dices que te pongan una limonada en la espalda, y me la traes, papito.

Y, créase o no, ahí, en el suelo, lo abofeteó otra vez.

A mí, de redentor que me esculquen, si quisiera salvar vidas usaría traje de baño; sin embargo, como alguien para quien esto es un oficio, creo que la violencia tiene su lugar y medida. Y aquel espectáculo era puro capricho que me estaba estropeando los molletes. Me levanté de mi asiento y dirigí mi diestra hacia la parte de atrás del pantalón para coger la pistola. Pero entonces feo malora hizo la seña secreta que identifica a los miembros de la organización; no de esa en la que chambeo y que me da fama y me da de comer, sino de La Organización. El doble parpadeo seguido de un breve rasquido detrás de la oreja izquierda. Volví a sentarme. Feo malora se fue detrás de modesto catrín en su camino a la cocina, propinándole puntapiés en el trasero. Entonces sucedió lo impensable. Modesto catrín me miró y, a continuación, también él hizo la seña secreta.

He brought his forehead in to meet diffident spiff's, without actually touching it, and delivered a whole-hand slap from the left. Diffident spiff stumbled leftward and had to grab hold of a chair to keep from falling.

Up to that point, the scene was exciting and only slightly uncomfortable, besides it was someone else's business. But ugly thug fired off another slap, calculated, downward, one of those half-cheek-half-ear smacks that sting and stun, and diffident spiff fell to the floor.

"Now, *just like that*, you go to the kitchen, and you tell them to put a lemonade on your back, and you bring it back to me, papi."

And, believe it or not, there, on the floor, he slapped him once more.

Well, I'm no savior, so when you need one don't look my way; if I wanted to save lives I'd be in swim trunks, but as someone who does this for a job, I think violence has its place and scale. And this little display was a pure conceit that was ruining my morning *molletes*. So I got up and slipped my right hand in the back of my pants to grab my gun. But then ugly thug gave the secret sign identifying members of the organization, not the one I work for, which gives me my reputation and the food on my table, but "The Organization." A double-blink followed by a quick scratch behind the right ear. I sat back down. Ugly thug trailed after diffident spiff on his way to the kitchen, delivering little

27

Todo miembro de La Organización sabe que ella está por encima de cualquier otra lealtad, y que en cuanto un Hermano se identifica no se le puede hacer daño; pero ahí, frente a mis ojos, un Hermano estaba humillando a otro. Perplejo y alebrestado, empuñé mi pistola y la amartillé bajo la mesa. Esto no debía estar sucediendo. Resolví que el error era mío, que yo había visto mal y sólo uno de ellos había hecho la seña secreta.

Pero cuál. Tenía razones para identificarme con cualquiera de los dos. Aunque modesto catrín era más el tipo de hombre que hacía parte de La Organización, feo malora podría ser la clase de Hermano que cumplía funciones de músculo (categoría a la yo pertenecía, mal que me supiera). Éste era el momento en el que debía solicitar una confirmación. Me aclaré la garganta una vez, hice una pausa, y luego tres veces seguidas.

Feo malora se volvió a mirarme, no con curiosidad ni temor, fue una mirada de reconocimiento; pero no respondió a mi segunda señal. Modesto catrín, en cambio, chasqueó la lengua dos veces seguidas, luego otra. No me quedaba opción, me levanté y apunté hacia feo malora, pero en el último instante la duda me impidió jalar del gatillo, levanté la pistola y le pegué con la cacha en la sien. Feo malora se desplomó, levanté del suelo a modesto catrín, consideré con melancolía mi desayuno, y salimos.

Al cabo de un par de cuadras de silencio, modesto catrín recuperó el aliento y dijo, acercándose a mi oído:

—Hay algo que tiene qué explicarme.

kicks to his backside. Then the unthinkable occurred. Diffident spiff looked at me and, immediately thereafter, he too gave the secret sign.

Every member of The Organization knows that it comes above any other loyalty, and that as soon as a Brother self-identifies, you must do him no harm; but there, before my eyes, was one Brother humiliating another. Baffled and keyed up, I grabbed my gun and cocked it under the table. This shouldn't be happening. I decided that it had been my mistake, that I'd seen wrong and only one of them had made the secret sign.

But which one. I had reasons to identify myself to either of them. Though diffident spiff seemed more the sort of man who formed part of The Organization, ugly thug could be the kind of Brother employed as muscle (the category I myself belonged to, distasteful as I might find it). This was the point at which I was to seek confirmation. I cleared my throat once, paused, then three times in a row.

Ugly thug turned to look at me, not in curiosity or fear, it was a look of recognition; but he didn't respond to my second signal. Diffident spiff, on the other hand, clucked his tongue twice in a row, then once more. I had no option, I got up and aimed at ugly thug, but at the last second doubt kept me from pulling the trigger and I raised the gun and clocked him in the temple with the grip. Ugly thug collapsed, I pulled diffident spiff from the floor, gazed wistfully at my breakfast, and we left.

After a couple blocks in silence, diffident spiff

Aprovechándose de la cercanía agarró la pistola que había vuelto a guardar en el pantalón y me apuntó.

—¿Por qué interrumpió la operación?

Más que por la amenaza del arma, me dejó frío la sorpresa.

—Tenía que haber dejado que él me pateara y luego yo me resistiera —continuó—, para que el Hermano disparara y matara al hombre de la mesa junto a la cocina: debía parecer un accidente. ¿Por qué no obedeció la seña indicándole que había una operación en curso?

—¿La seña?

—Con el dedo meñique, me rasqué la oreja con el dedo meñique, no con el índice. Debía haber entendido entonces. Y después chasqueé la lengua tres veces seguidas, luego otra, que es la señal de retirada. Me parece muy sospechoso que no haya entendido ninguna de las dos señales.

—¿Tres veces? ¿no dos?

—Tres —insistió— ¿Puede explicar su comportamiento?

Resignado, suspiré y, para variar, decidí reconocer la verdad, aunque ello marcara mi futuro dentro de La Organización:

—Sólo soy un músculo.

Modesto catrín me observó detenidamente —creo que hasta con piedad—, y dijo "Claro", pero no hizo ademán de devolverme la pistola.

caught his breath and said, leaning in to my ear, "There's something you have to explain."

Taking advantage of our proximity he grabbed the gun I'd tucked back into my trousers and aimed it at me.

"Why did you interrupt the operation?"

More than the threat of the weapon, it was the shock that chilled me.

"You were supposed to let him kick me and then let me fight back," he went on, "so the Brother could shoot and kill the man at the table by the kitchen: *it was supposed to look like an accident.* Why didn't you obey the sign for operation in progress?"

"The sign?"

"My pinkie. I scratched my ear with my pinkie, not my index finger. You must have caught that. Then I clucked my tongue three times in a row, then once more, the sign to retreat. I think it's very suspicious that you didn't catch either of those signals."

"Three times? Not twice?"

"Three," he insisted. "Can you explain your behavior?"

Resigned, I sighed and decided, for a change, to admit the truth, even if it marked my future in The Organization.

"I'm just muscle."

Diffident spiff observed me carefully—I think even with pity—and said, "Right," but made no move to give back my gun.

31

HYGGE

DORTHE NORS

S å sad vi der, Lilly og mig, og hun havde lavet kaffe og bagt en chokoladekage af dem, der er bløde i midten. I løbet af eftermiddagen, havde hun også fået støvsuget, og tørret de døde blade af vindueskarmene. Undulaten snakkede ikke længere med fra sit bur, men var stedt til hvile under et viskestykke, og i fjernsynet var der noget, vi kunne gætte med på. Da jeg var forbi i eftermiddags, havde det ikke været så pænt. Vi havde haft et udfald om hendes facon, måden hun skabte sig på, når vi var i seniorklubben, hendes jalousi og hendes sødme, der stik imod hensigten virker forrående. Og så sagde hun det

HYGGE

DORTHE NORS

TRANSLATED BY MISHA HOEKSTRA

Then we were sitting there, Lilly and me, and she had made coffee and baked one of those chocolate cakes that are soft in the middle. During the afternoon she'd also vacuumed and cleared the dead leaves off the windowsills. The budgie was no longer chattering in its cage, it had been put under a dish towel to rest, and on the tube there was some show we could guess along with. When I'd come by in the afternoon, it hadn't been so nice. We had a falling out about her manner, about the way she'd act up when we were at the senior club, her jealousy and her sweetness, which to me seemed vulgar. And then she'd said that business about my

der med mit ansigt. At hun ikke kunne lide det. *Dig og dit lektorfjæs*, sagde hun, og vasketøjet havde ligget på gulvet i badeværelset og flydt. Hun havde ikke redt sengen, og der lugtede sødt af urin. Jeg kender den lugt fra tante Claras hjem, dengang hun ikke længere kunne se, og famlede rundt og væltede alting, særligt sig selv. Det var, som om noget dødt havde taget permanent ophold i kroppens celler, og nu løb ud sammen med toiletbesøgene. Den slags satte sig i tapeterne, og lugten var der, når vi skulle hygge os med det saftevand, jeg selv kunne blande ude i køkkenet. Disse lange eftermiddage med fad saft, pebermyntebolsjer og tante Clara, der ikke længere passede til sine tænder. Der er ting, man ikke glemmer; måden vi sang af sangbogen på og hendes transskriberinger af Kongens nytårstaler for eksempel, og jeg har aldrig forstået, hvorfor jeg skulle tages som gidsel af tante Claras ensomhed. Hvorfor krævede den min involvering. Jeg var kun en dreng, og mens jeg sad der og blev lagt Kong Frederiks ord i munden, var mine forældre velsagtens i biografen. *Du er så dygtig i skolen*, sagde de. *Den slags skal stimuleres*, sagde de, og så var tante Clara der med sine lærerindefingre i min nakke. Skålen med sukkerknalder op under ansigtet: *Tag én min dreng, tag to, spis!*

Men nu havde hun lavet kaffe, Lilly, hun havde lavet kaffe, og hun havde dækket undulaten til og fundet sine pæne kopper frem. Der var ikke mere noget

face   that she didn't like it. "You and your big professor mug," she'd said. The floor in the bathroom was
littered with laundry. She hadn't made the bed either,
and there was that sweetish smell of urine. I know that
smell from Aunt Marguerite's home, back when she
could no longer see and fumbled around and knocked
everything over, especially herself. It was as if something had taken up permanent residence in her cells,
and now it oozed out on her trips to the toilet and settled into the wallpaper. The odor was there when we sat
down to enjoy the fruit drink that I mixed up out in her
kitchen. Those long afternoons with flat fruit drink,
peppermint candies, and Aunt Marguerite, whose teeth
no longer fit her. There are some things you never forget: the way we sang from the songbook, for instance,
and her transcriptions of the king's speeches on New
Year's Eve. I've never understood why I should have
been hostage to Aunt Marguerite's loneliness, why it
demanded my involvement. I was just a boy, and while
I sat there and had King Frederik's words placed in my
mouth, I suppose my folks were at the movie theater.
"You're so clever in school," they'd say. "That sort of
thing needs stimulation," they'd say, and then Aunt
Marguerite would be there with her schoolmarm fingers on my neck, the bowl with sugar cubes up in my
face: "Take one, my boy, take two, eat them!"

35

But now Lilly was making the coffee and had covered the budgie and gotten out the nice cups. There

med mit ansigt. Mit ansigt, mine hænder og mine knæ, alt fandt hun kælent. Hendes lille hånd var oppe i mit hår, inde ved min bukselinning, min hånd ville hun have fat i, for *nu skulle vi hygge, vi skulle have det rigtigt hyggeligt, ja, og ikke snakke mere om det.* Men siden jeg første gang mødte hende i seniorklubben er hendes ansigt blevet mere og mere en grød. Det er, som om én version er ved at vige for en anden, jeg kan stadig se den oprindelige, og det er ækelt, hvordan den ikke vil blive hængende. Det var Apotekeren, der fik mig med i klubben, han påstod, at vi skulle spille skak, men som ugift måtte jeg lægge krop til de aflagte kvinders forventninger. Så havde jeg en sok, de skulle ordne, så var der noget med mit kravetøj, og så fik de ondt i fødderne og ville gerne køres hjem. Blandt de desperate var Lilly en ener. Først prøvede hun sig på Apotekeren, men de andre kvinder var om ham som hyæner om et kadaver. Det var hans flotte skæg, sagde hun, og man kan sikkert sige en del godt om Lilly, men de fantasifulde bluser, kan ikke dække over det ufravigelige. Al den pynt, ja, selv undulaten, trækker hende kun ned, og så sad vi der, det var i lørdags, og der var jo fyrfadslys. Ovre på reolen havde hun stillet dem ud på kanten, og hun havde bukket stanniol omkring dem forneden, så de ikke kunne brænde ned i laminatet. Det var sket for hende før; at fyrfadslysene var brændt ned i laminatet, og hun havde også oplevet dem eksplodere. Væsken i de små

wasn't any more talk about my face. My face, my hands, my knees—now she found everything cuddly. Her little hand up in my hair, inside the waist of my trousers, she wanted to grab hold of me, "Because now we're going to enjoy ourselves, we're going to have us a cozy time, yeah, and not talk about it anymore." Since I first met her in the senior club, her face has gotten more and more porridgy. It's as if one version has started to give way to another, I can still see the original, and it's awful how it won't stick around. It was the druggist who got me into the club, he claimed that we'd play chess, but as a bachelor I had to place my body at the disposal of the castoff women and their expectations. I had a sock they needed to see to, there was something about my collar, their feet started hurting and they wanted to be driven home. Among the desperate, Lilly stood out. First she tried to latch on to the druggist, but the other women were on him like hyenas around a cadaver. It was his fine beard, she said. No doubt you can say some good things about Lilly, but those fancy blouses can't cover up what can't be changed. All that frippery, yes, the budgie, too, it only drags her down, and now we were sitting there, it was Saturday and the tea candles were lit. She had placed them along the edge of the bookcase, with tinfoil wrapped around the bases so they wouldn't burn down into the laminate. It had happened to her before—that the tea lights had burned into the laminate or exploded. The liquid wax could

bægre kunne blive antændelig som benzin, så hun
var mest tryg ved de lange lys. De statelige. Dem var
man, hvis man ikke stillede dem op ad gardinet, mere
sikre på. *De er lidt ligesom dig*, fnisede hun, *så ranke og
ordentlige i det*, sagde hun og kantede sig op af sofaen
og videre ud i køkkenet, hvor hun rumsterede. *Men
når bare vi holder os vågne, så går det nok med de små!*
råbte hun derudefra, og jeg har tit tænkt på, at Lilly
er en af dem, der let kan komme til at falde i søvn
med en cigaret. Hun kunne falde hen på sofaen, under
billederne af de solblegede pårørende. Der hænger
også et af Lilly selv fra engang i halvfjerdserne. Hun
har håret bukket med krøllejern på den måde, mine
studerende også bukkede deres dengang. Så kunne
de sidde der og gøre sig attraktive, mens jeg sloges
med deres sløset tegnede logaritmer. Hvis de da ikke
dinglede rundt på deres alt for høje espadrilles, som
havde de bundet halmballer under fødderne, herre-
gud, og deres shampoo stank i klasselokalet, når den
blev blandet med lugten af armhuler og skød. De sav-
nede værdighed, men juleafslutningerne var trods alt
de værste. Æbleskiverne og gløggen, for så skulle der
hygges, og man skulle snakke om året, der var gået.
Som om året kunne andet. Som om det ikke præcis er
sådan, tiden er indstillet, og Lilly har også skolebil-
leder hængende af sin bedagede yngel. Der er noget
med deres ansigter, noget melbolleagtigt, blødt. De
har fået alt for meget slik, de børn, og nu bor de i en

get to be as flammable as gasoline, so she felt safer with tapers. The dignified sort. So long as you didn't set them up against the curtains, you could count on them. "They're a bit like you," she giggled, "so orderly and erect," she said, scooting her way off the couch and out into the kitchen, where I could hear her rummaging around. "But if we can just stay awake, the little ones should be fine!" she shouted. I've often thought that Lilly's one of those who could easily fall asleep with a cigarette in her hand. I could see her doing that on the couch, beneath the sun-faded pictures of her relatives. There was one hanging there of Lilly too, from sometime in the seventies. She's got her hair crimped with an iron, the way my students crimped theirs back then. They would sit there, trying to make themselves attractive while I struggled with their sloppy logarithm assignments. That is, if they weren't tottering around on those espadrilles that were way too high, as if they'd attached hay bales under their feet, good Lord, their shampoo stinking in the classroom, mixing with the stench of armpits and sex. They lacked dignity, and the last day before Christmas break was always the worst. The fried doughnut holes and mulled wine, because we were supposed to hang out and talk about the year that had passed. As if the year could do anything else. As if that's not precisely the way time works.

Lilly had school pictures of her aging offspring on the wall as well. There was something about their

anden sidegade i det samme kvarter, med deres børn,
som også er for fede, men det kan man jo ikke sige til
Lilly. Hun føler ingenting det meste af tiden, men der
skal ingenting til, så føler hun alt, og så kom hun side-
læns ind ad døren med en bakke. *Vi skal have Bailey
til kaffen*, sagde hun. Bailey og nogle pebermynter,
hun havde til overs fra jul. *Vi skal have det lidt godt*,
sagde hun, og så klemte hun sig ned ved siden af mig
i sofaen; hendes fingre med de hedengangne vielses-
ringe, og denne klirren af ametyst og andre former for
simili fra hendes øreflipper. Vel er hun tilforladelig,
det er varmeblus det hele, jeg ved det, og Apotekeren
siger det også, men Bailey smager af tysk rasteplads
og det hjørne af festen, hvor der ingenting sker. I øv-
rigt burde Lilly antage, at jeg var mere til whisky.
Eller en tør cognac med en cigar. Jeg vil spille skak.
Jeg er ingens efeb, og tro ikke, at jeg ikke ved, hvad
hun har under håndvasken og ude ved elmåleren,
Clara. Jeg kender alt til likøren nede fra købmanden
på hjørnet, og den er ved at sylte hendes ansigt, den
har lagt hendes tunge i lage. Mig kan hun ikke skjule
noget for. Jeg har kendt hende i en menneskealder, og
jeg kan ikke løbes om hjørner med længere. Men det
var, mens vi begge sad i sofaen, mig med hendes løse
hånd på bukseknæet, og hun med blikket på Baileyen,
at hun sagde: *Vi er da gode venner*, sagde hun. *Jeg ved
også godt, jeg er dum, og det kan ikke være let for dig med
din viden at trække rundt med sådan en som mig*, sagde

faces, something dumplingish and soft. They had too much candy, those kids, and now they're living on another side street in the same neighborhood with kids of their own, kids who are also too fat, not to put too fine a point on it, but that's not something you could tell Lilly. She doesn't feel anything, most of the time, but it takes nothing at all to make her feel everything, and then she was sidling through the door with a tray. "We're having Baileys with coffee," she said, Baileys and some peppermints she had leftover from Christmas. "We're going to have a nice little time," she said, and then she squeezed herself in next to me on the couch, her fingers with the defunct wedding band, and the jingle of amethyst and other costume jewels dangling from her earlobes. I guess she's harmless enough, it's all just heat. I know that and the druggist says the same, but Baileys tastes of German rest areas and the corner of some party where nothing's happening. Besides, Lilly should have been able to work out that I'm more one for whiskey. Or a dry cognac with a cigar. I want to play chess! I'm nobody's pet, and don't think I don't know what she had under the sink or out by the electric meter, Marguerite. I know all about the liquor from the corner grocer's, it was starting to pickle her tongue. She can't hide anything from me. I've known her for a dog's age, and I can't be led around by the nose anymore. But it was while we were both sitting on the couch, me with her free

hun. *Så skal vi nu ikke bare hygge os.* Og det gjorde vi
så. Vi sad der og hyggede os, og jeg kan ikke rede-
gøre for passagen imellem, at hun tog den sidste bid
af kagen, og så at hun lå dernede på gulvet, halvt inde
under stuebordet, øjnene åbne, munden også, men
selv der, da det hele var forbi, så det ud, som om hun
var i gang med at nøde mig, ja, hun nødede mig, og
jeg ville ikke.

hand on my trouser knee and her with her eye on the Baileys, that she said, "We're good friends, aren't we? I know I'm stupid," she said, "and it can't be easy for you with all your brains to go around with someone like me," she said. "So can't we just be cozy?" And so we were. We sat there and were cozy, and I can't account for how we got from the moment she took the last bite of cake to her lying there on the floor, halfway under the coffee table, eyes gawping, mouth, too, but even then, when it all was over and done, it felt as though she were forcing me, yes, she forced me, and I didn't like it.

EXIT INTERVIEW

CHRISTIAN HAYDEN

Well, Tony, I'm glad we got this out of the way, as unpleasant as it was. I'm sorry we had to do it over the phone, but we really couldn't risk you coming back to the office.

. . .

It's never fun to dissolve a partnership, Tony, particularly one as fruitful as ours has been. But you have been a valuable asset to Healthcare Solutional Results over the years, and we wish you the best of—

. . .

What?

. . .

I see.

. . .

Yes. Well. Let me say categorically that I deny these allegations, for you and for whomever else might be listening in.

. . .

Sure there aren't, Tony.

. . .

Look, Tony, if there was a breach of sensitive material, if millions of electronic health records were stolen and sold to a variety of drug manufacturers, health-care marketing firms, and Chinese actuarial betting syndicates, then it was conducted without my knowledge, and in fact I'm shocked and dismayed to hear it.

. . .

You're asking me what a Chinese actuarial betting syndicate is? Didn't you bring that up?

. . .

Fine, fine. I guess I brought it up.

. . .

I don't know if I should say.

. . .

I'm going to speak in purely theoretical terms, okay? Purely theoretical. I got this information from an article I read in *Vice*. It might not even be real. I can never tell if those are real or not.

. . .

Anyway. What I read is that there is a gambling ring, based in China, for rich people to bet on the life spans of others.

. . .

Well, essentially they pick a random person, usually an older person. They gather some information and then they put an over-under on them reaching sixty, seventy, eighty, etc.

. . .

Age, obviously. Country of residence. Smoker/nonsmoker. That sort of thing.

. . .

Right. So maybe you get a seventy-three-year-old American. There's an 80 percent chance he'll live to seventy-four. So you place a hundred-dollar bet that he'll die in a year, wait that year, and if he lives you lose. If he dies you pocket four hundred bucks.

. . .

The bets are much bigger in real life. Nobody waits twelve months for four hundred bucks. I'm talking tens of thousands of dollars, if not more.

. . .

Can you really not put that together, Tony? Really? This is why you were dismissed from the board.

. . .

Where am I? I'm in the off—Oh, I see. I see your game. I'm overseas. I'm not saying where.

. . .

I'll have you know I'm rerouting this phone call through a series of proxy phone numbers. BEE-BOOP-BEE-BOOP! Hear that? That's me sending the call to Pakistan or Bulgaria or wherever the fuck I want it to go. You can't find me.

. . .

I am *not* at the office. I'm just making it look like I am. Fuck it—tell these FBI guys to kick down the office doors! They'll see I'm not there.

. . .

Oh, really? They don't need a warrant if I tell them to kick in the doors? I retract that. I retract that. Don't kick down the doors, SEC or FBI or whoever you are.

. . .

You know what I think? I think the minute you got the boot you ran crying to whichever government agency was willing to give you immunity. Though why you'd need immunity in the first place, I have no idea.

. . .

I *should* hang up. But I feel a little bad, Tony, because this is your exit interview and it would be kind of déclassé to hang up on you while you're trying to leave gracefully. Plus, why should I hang up? I have nothing to hide. Plus, I'm in the Maldives. Or am I, assholes?

. . .

Okay.

. . .

Yeah, you're pretty dense, Tony. Just an FYI. This is part of why you were kicked off the board. You really can't make that connection?

. . .

Think about it. If I'm betting on a man's life, it would be pretty fucking great if I had his health records, wouldn't it? Let's run through the same scenario as before. There's a guy, seventy-three, should live to seventy-four, no problem—but oh wait, he's got Stage IV non-small-cell lung carcinoma. Survival rate drops to 5 percent. Pretty good bet, right?

. . .

So that is *why* a Chinese actuarial betting syndicate would theoretically want access to the health records of millions of people, Tony. Now, if you or your esteemed colleagues at the Justice Department are wondering *how* an actuarial betting syndicate got ahold of the health records of millions of people . . . I can't help you there. It wasn't through my shop. Wasn't through Healthcare Solutional Results. And if documents come to light showing that it was through Healthcare Solutional Results, then those documents will also undoubtedly show that I personally had nothing to do with it.

. . .

Just because I'm the founder and CEO of Healthcare Solutional Results doesn't mean I know everything that's going on with the entire company. You know my style—I'm a macromanager.

. . .

"Solutional" is too a word, Tony. Add this to the list of reasons you were voted off the board: wouldn't go with the flow. Everyone else liked Solutional. We create solutions. Therefore, we are solutional.

. . .

You're really harping on the Chinese actuarial betting syndicates. I should send you that *Vice* article.

. . .

Right. Yeah. That would be sort of like the seamy underbelly of Chinese actuarial betting syndicates. Sometimes you're $20K in the hole on a sweet little ninety-seven-year-old Belarusian. Two percent chance he'll reach ninety-eight. But uh-oh. It's a week until his birthday and he's still kicking. Rides a bicycle every day. Eats nothing but leafy greens. Looks like you're out twenty grand. Unless . . . you make some calls. You get in touch with the local Belarusian criminal element. You pay $5K for a "bike accident." Get my drift?

. . .

Or the other way around. You put $100K on a thirty-nine-year-old, hundred-to-one shot, and then you arrange for him to get polonium poisoning or whatever. Pay a million bucks for it; you still come out ahead. Not that I've ever done anything like that.

. . .

Hang on, Tony, I'm getting in the car. Give me a minute—I have to pull out on this tough hill.

. . .

No, it is *not* the tough hill right in front of the office. It's a tough hill in Peru. Maybe.

. . .

Okay, back.

. . .

As a matter of fact I *am* thirty-nine.

. . .

Well, that's a pretty stupid bet, Tony, since I'm a pescatarian and I elliptical eight miles every goddamn day. But, sure, waste your money. This is another reason you got dropped, T. Stupid financial decisions.

. . .

Hmm? Sorry, I'm a little distracted. It's the weirdest thing. My brakes don't seem to be working at all and—Oh, you son of a bitch, Tony. You son of a bitch. You're going to rue the day, my friend. You're going to rue the day you fucked with

RATFACE

PAUL LA FARGE

The next to last time I saw Polanski, he told me he had incurable stomach cancer and he was going to France to die. His rat face was set in an angry droop. "That way I won't bother anybody," he said. "I'll just die on my own." I wondered who he was afraid of bothering. His wife had left him, and as far as I knew he didn't have kids. I'd seen him once with a little black dog, but that was years ago, and if it was still alive I figured it had ended up with his ex-wife. "What are you going to do in France?" I asked. "Does it matter?" Polanski said. "I'll work in a bookstore until they put me in the hospital. Or I'll just sleep on the bank of a canal." I didn't know if he was serious or not, but I said I hoped he would be all right. He wrapped up the copy of Nabokov's *Glory* I'd found on the shelf for an astounding eight bucks, and I went out.

Later I heard that Polanski had cleaned out Brewer's business checking account: fifty thousand dollars, which Brewer had earmarked for a renovation. He wrote himself a check and deposited it, and by the time Brewer noticed, Polanski was gone. The money put another light on his cancer story. Though in a way, not really. If all Polanski wanted was to steal Brewer's money and disappear, there was no need for him to tell me anything. Probably he *did* have cancer, I thought, and he'd gone to France for a final spree. I imagined him staying in grand hotels, drinking champagne. A girl on each arm, and Polanski twitching between them, like a rat that doesn't know which button delivers the electric shock. The whole scene shot through with the sadness of what was happening in his stomach.

Brewer went out of business, so I bought my books at Nautilus, on the other side of the park. They had fewer bargains, but, on the other hand, a girl named Lisa worked there on Saturday and Sunday afternoons. We talked about Kafka, about James Thurber. We got married and had a kid. Ten years passed, for me a happy period, although I sometimes had the feeling that I was standing with my feet on either side of a fast-moving stream, which was washing away everything I knew. It was only a matter of time before I fell into it and got washed away in turn. Then I'd look up and absolutely nothing was wrong. To no one's surprise, our kid was turning out to be a reader. He sat at dinner with his face in a book. Lisa and I agreed it wasn't a problem, but we told him he'd have to put the book down before he learned to drive. "I'm never going to learn to drive," he said. "Just wait," I said. "You don't know what's coming." He said he did, he'd read about it already. We couldn't have loved him more than we did.

In 1988, the Monday after Thanksgiving, there was a gas explosion at his school. The fire department saved nearly everyone, but not our kid. He'd locked himself in a faculty bathroom; by the time they broke the door down he was dead from smoke inhalation. We buried him next to Lisa's parents, in a field off the highway. Lisa stayed out there and I went back to the city. The apartment was like a frozen mastodon, impossible to change, impossible to keep the way it was. That winter lasted five years. Then it was spring; trees were budding outside the window. I went to the park to read. I was just thinking that life was completely unreal, that there were no banks to stand on but also no stream rushing past, and that if you had to say what the truth of life was, you would say that nothing ever really happens, when this guy walks by with a little black dog. I look up and say, "Polanski?"

He's decades older, but of the two of us, he's the less aged. He leans down to shake my hand. "What are you doing here?" I ask. He asks if I can keep a secret.

"Sure," I say. There's nobody I could tell. Polanski says he never had cancer. He never went to France, either. All this time, he's been living around the corner. He spent Brewer's money, and when it was gone he got a job at another bookshop, then another. "I don't get it," I say. Polanski smiles like he's not surprised. "You book people never do," he says. He lets me pat his dog. It tries to jump up on my lap, but Polanski tells it to behave and the two of them move on.

MARY WHEN YOU FOLLOW HER

CARMEN MARIA MACHADO

In the autumn of Maria's eighteenth year, the year that her beloved father—amateur coin collector, retired auto worker, lapsed Catholic—died silently of liver cancer three weeks after his diagnosis, and the autumn her favorite dog killed her favorite cat on the brown, crisped grass of their front lawn, and the cold came so early that the apples on the trees froze and fell like stones dropped from heaven, and the fifth local Dominican teenager in as many months disappeared while walking home from her minimum-wage, dead-end job, leaving behind a kid sister and an unfinished journal and a bedroom in her mother's house she'd never made enough to leave—deepening the community's collective paroxysm of anxiety, which made them yell at their daughters and give out abstruse and non-sensical advice about how to avoid being a victim and boosted the sales of pepper spray and Saint Anthony pendants, and also prompted no action from the police, who said that the girls were likely runaways—the same autumn she finally figured out how to give herself an orgasm, right after the summer when she broke up with her boyfriend of two years, Ira, who had for their entire relationship been attempting to make her come with the grim determination of a pioneer woman churning butter and had failed one hundred percent of the time, and she got herself one of those minimum-wage, dead-end jobs because she was saving for a one-way bus ticket to Chicago, and she was finally hired at Phil's Discount restocking cheap T-shirts and over-stock home goods, and learned quickly to evade Phil's hands, which always seemed to brush against her body when the two of them passed each other in the bowels of the store, which is also the same autumn that Maria had started taking a shortcut home at night—in spite of her mother's warnings—through the unlit parking lot of the bankrupt, half-gutted strip mall where she'd once bought her quinceañera dress, and listened to the leaves rasping over the pavement and watched an owl dismember a mouse on the pavement and then slipped her Walkman's headphones over her ears even though her mother had warned her that music would conceal an attacker's approaching footsteps, and felt her ponytail bouncing against the back of her neck even though her mother had warned her that a ponytail was little more than a handle for rapists, and felt thrilled to her trembling core much in the same way she felt when her orgasms ebbed away, and after she had gone to a party held in a foreclosed house and drank deeply of syrupy, mysterious liquids in paper cups and talked about the missing girls with Dolores and Perdita, whose own parents had forbidden them to walk alone or go out at night, and after her mother's shitty station wagon broke down twenty miles away from home when she'd been on an errand to refill her brother's asthma medication and she had to hitchhike back in the passenger seat of an eighteen wheeler while chatting manically to fill the dangerous silence, and after she went home with a co-worker who sort of looked like Ira and smelled a bit like him too (because even though Ira'd been bad at sex and kissing and so many other things besides, she'd found his presence comforting and stable and missed him a little), and after that co-worker turned out to have a foot fetish and wanted to rub his erect dick all over Maria's boots and Maria let him because she didn't know what would happen if she didn't, and after she tried to clean them off with fallen leaves in that unlit parking lot of the bankrupt, half-gutted strip mall and while hunched over her project heard the sound of someone walking toward her with exquisite patience, and she didn't look back but bolted like a deer

59

and in her socks, leaving her boots (her favorite pair!) behind, and after Perdita showed up at her front door on a Sunday morning because Dolores had gone missing, too, and they'd searched and searched and eventually found Dolores's keys in a ditch next to the road next to the elementary school but never anything else, and after Phil handed her a paycheck with his other hand shoved deeply into his pocket and didn't let go right away when she tried to take the envelope, and after Maria told him to go fuck himself and he shoved her against the OSHA poster and called her a bitch and told her he'd let her keep her job under one condition, and after she ran home through the unlit parking lot of the bankrupt, half-gutted strip mall and looked up as she ran hoping to see a cathedral of stars but instead just saw a terrible darkness, and after she snapped at her mother that she was fine and collapsed in her bedroom wheezing and crying and then overturned her father's old cigar box and counted her money, but months before a white girl from a rich neighborhood also disappeared and suddenly the police were combing through the snarled streets in full force and Maria's mother said that she wished Maria was around to see them finally doing their jobs, and before the town was buried under four feet of snow, which no one could deny gave them a strange sense of relief, a sense that time's terrible, ticking advancement had been stilled for a spell, and before a snowplow operator accidentally uncovered the shallow graves and their bodies near the unlit parking lot of the bankrupt, half-gutted strip mall, and before they arrested the high school chemistry teacher and the community demanded answers, and before they learned that they would never, ever get them, Maria left a note for her mother on the fridge telling her that she loved her and was sorry and missed her already, and as she sat on the bus to Chicago, her backpack in her lap and her rosary coiled in her coat pocket and the windows smeared with someone else's face grease, she imagined that the missing girls were all living in the city in brick row houses on a single block, a well-lit block with gardens and parks and a sidewalk, where they all laughed and made art and dated and dined and fucked and danced and aged and married and had children, and at night told stories to each other about the last, long-ago time they'd truly been afraid.

GHOST LIGHT

ELIZABETH HAND

I was never a fan of Zeke McDermott's music. Too angsty, despite the Tom Waits growl and lumberjack look favored by guys who wouldn't know a maul from a mailbox. He wasn't famous enough to sell out the Burnt Harbor Opera House, or get booked in summer, when the big names come through.

But he might well have sold out if he'd had the chance to play in July rather than February. He had buzz—solid Pitchfork rankings, an NPR feature. Still not my taste, though a lot of people here like his stuff. Once the foodies started migrating north from Brooklyn and Boston, the Opera House drew a younger demographic. When McDermott came through last winter, the house was half-full, damn good considering the show had been canceled due to a blizzard, then rescheduled for two nights later.

McDermott didn't travel with a road crew. Few solo performers do unless they're a name—that's why places like the Opera House hire guys like me to run lights and sound. McDermott rode out the storm at the Harbor Inn, in what passes for downtown. That was when he hooked up with Bree. Bree lives above the Rum Line, across from the Opera House. Bree's cute, small, and tomboyish, with a fish tattoo on her upper arm, a brookie. I assumed she was gay. I never caught any sexual vibe from her, not so unusual when you consider I'm twice her age, a former roadie who drives to Ellsworth to attend weekly NarcAnon meetings.

Anyway, she met McDermott at the Rum Line. They spent the next three nights together. My place is a few doors down from the Inn; I saw her leaving a couple times. I wasn't stalking her: that's just the kind of thing you notice in a town small as this.

Plus, Bree works for me. She went to Northeastern to study music—she plays mandolin—but moved back home after a year. Money issues. I know her dad and, as a favor, took her under my wing. Taught her the basics of wiring, how to rig the lighting pipes, set up and break down a show. How to check the ropes, which were sisal and prone to fray. Bigger venues like the Camden Opera House have updated their tech. Burnt Harbor can't afford that, so we make do.

Bree was good at it. I ended up hiring her. I liked having her around, liked hearing her play the mandolin while I figured out lighting cues. Far as I know, she never slept with the talent till McDermott. Didn't matter to me as long as she did her job.

And all bets are off during a blizzard. She showed up on the afternoon of the rescheduled performance, and we got to work.

That was a magical gig. People were stir crazy after the storm, not a full house but enthusiastic. McDermott had a strong stage presence. Good-looking enough, with a beard and dark hair, a disarmingly gruff, somewhat theatrical manner at odds with all those heartachy songs. He sat in a chair near the edge of the stage, cradling his Gibson as he sang into a mic that dated to the Nixon era.

His only special request was he wanted a floor lamp within reach. He did this shtick during his closer, something else he copped from Waits: set down his guitar and danced, did this little drunken waltz with the mic, singing as he grabbed on to the lamp like an old-time cartoon drunk. Our lamp had a tasseled shade and had done hard duty in community theater plays for decades. Blue gels in the follow spot simulated moonlight; dust in the air glowed like snow. Schmaltzy but effective. He got a standing ovation.

To top it off, he brought Bree and her mandolin onstage for an encore. I don't know if they planned it or not. Not, I think, from the way she blushed. They sang "Shady Grove," the two of them grinning at each other like they'd done this a hundred times.

I know they were together that night—next day was one of the few when Bree showed up late for work. I didn't say anything. She looked happier than I'd ever seen her.

That didn't last. Weeks went by, then months. She never told me, but I knew. She gained a little weight, then lost it, showed up a few times drunk or stoned. I reamed her out—it wasn't just unprofessional but dangerous. I didn't want one of those pipes falling on me, or her.

After that I'd still see her at the Rum Line, but she showed up sober. Never heard her play the mandolin again.

A year went by. Come February, McDermott's back. No blizzard this time: freakishly warm weather, no snow, maple sap running. I called McDermott and asked if he wanted anything special.

Nope. Like last year, just a mic and standing lamp close to hand.

Bree laid down spike tape to mark where his chair and mic would go. The lamp we'd used before had been totaled during a production of *Arsenic and Old Lace*, so we used the ghost light. That's a safety precaution required for theaters: a standing lamp with a naked bulb that's turned on after hours, when the house is dark.

Our ghost light was old, like everything else. Bree measured off from McDermott's chair, set the lamp there. We were good to go.

We didn't sell out, but it was close. Locals remembered last year's show, and the springlike weather brought people from far away as Bangor. Inside, it must've been eighty degrees, worse onstage with the footlights. I'd asked Bree to turn down the heat; either she forgot or so many bodies raised the temp.

Still, McDermott put on a great show. When it came time for his final song, I dimmed everything save for that spooky blue follow spot. He waltzed around with the mic, sweat streaming down his face: a convincing drunk. Did his little pirouette and grabbed the ghost light.

It looked like part of the act. His head snapped back: he clutched the mic in one hand and the lamp in the other, staggering to the edge of the stage. Some people laughed.

Then he plummeted offstage, pulling mic stand and lamp with him. People screamed. Somebody—Bree, probably—hit the houselights. Somebody else called 911.

Probably he was dead before he hit the floor. From the lighting booth, I could see how his neck torqued as his head struck the stage edge. I raced down, yelling at people to get away in case the mic and ghost light were still live. Fortunately, the cords were yanked out as he fell.

I dealt with the cops and EMTs when they arrived, and later with more cops. So did Bree. Everyone knew me, everyone believed me when I said I'd checked everything beforehand. With all that antiquated equipment, I'd invested in a good continuity tester and a Klein Non-Contact Voltage Tester. I went around before every show, twice, making sure nothing was hot—that none of the lights or equipment had a live current. I'd done that as usual before McDermott's gig.

The death was ruled accidental. No one blamed me, or Bree, but the Opera House was shuttered afterwards and we had to find other work. Neither of us spoke to any media, though videos of Bree playing with McDermott showed up online, along with footage from his final show.

I know what happened. That old ghost light had a two-prong plug that wasn't polarized like modern ones. If you plugged it into the wall outlet one way, no problem. If you put it in with the prongs reversed, the metal lampstand would be live with current. Even that wasn't a problem—unless you grasped the lamp with one hand and something else that was grounded with the other. Like a mic.

Bree knew to plug in the ghost light so it wasn't hot. And I'd checked it, twice. At some point before the performance, she'd gone backstage, yanked the plug then put it back in, reversed so the ghost light was live.

If you brush a hot piece of equipment with your

knuckles, you'll get a shock, though not enough to kill you. If you grab it, the live current causes your muscles to contract: you can't let go. Combine that with sweaty hands, a grounded mic, a dim stage, and an eight-foot drop, and you get Zeke McDermott, RIP.

I never said anything to Bree about it. I assume she had her reasons. She's taken up the mandolin again—I see her sometimes at the Rum Line's open mic night. She's pretty damn good.

HIGHWAY ONE

BENJAMIN WHITMER

'm tripping balls, the coldest fucking night of the year. We got the acid from Manny. We always do. Manny lives in one of the houses back over in the new development. It's one of those that went up in six weeks and makes no fucking sense. A Cape Cod next to a Victorian next to a California bungalow, all different colors. Toon Town we call it. Manny's got no reason being around us, never, and he never sleeps with us down by the river. His game's fucking the girls like Eli. It's why he comes down on Friday with beer, or, say, a sheet of acid.

"I got something to show you," Roth says. His dreadlocks are trying to blow in the wind down the alley, and his eyes're black, all pupil. He's grinning at me like the time I caught him in the library park watching two cats fuck, eating M&M's and rubbing his dick through his jeans.

This piece of shit. I hate smoking weed with Roth because he's always trying to fuck with you, and this is eleven hits of Highway One. The alley's night-shadows are breathing, everything's pulsing. It's cold enough I can't barely feel my fingers, but the muddy-smelling wind off the river is something you could lay back on and take a nap. "You don't have anything I need to see."

He holds his hand out to me. I have to squint, the way the moonlight filters down through the buildings. It's a pack of Pall Mall cigarettes, closed, the cellophane intact. And next to it, also in his hand, a single Pall Mall cigarette.

"Horseshit," I say. "Fuck you."

"Look," he says.

"I don't need to look." But I'm standing there staring at his hand, everything photograph-grainy. I can't move, the motherfucker.

"It must have fell out," he says. "But how?"

"Horseshit. It didn't fall out. You got it out somehow."

"How?" That cat-fucking grin on his face.

"I don't give a fuck."

He squints at me. "Don't be cunty. Manny's fucking that bitch. He's got her bent over a dumpster, beating that pussy."

He's talking about Eli. She just showed up this morning. Comes from some small town in Michigan where they make baby food, is what she told me. That's all I know. That and she carries a hammer in her bag, flapping around on her side with some clothes and a bunch of worry dolls.

I found her sparechanging out front of the toy store. A good place to sparechange, especially around Christmas. Works best when you look like Eli, too, almost a kid yourself. A thin little face, brown eyes that'll reach in your purse and find every nickel. I was smoking a Drum-rolled cigarette with her when one of the new cops walked by and saw the hammer too. "What're you planning on hammering?" he asked her.

She was smoking her cigarette, the one I rolled her. When she looked up at him, you could see the cop go weak-kneed. Her eyes'd do that to you, out from under the hood of her winter coat. "Nails," she said.

"Nails," he repeated. Then I swear the motherfucker blushed, and he walked away down towards the hardware store.

"You should come down by the river," I said to her.

73

"What's down by the river?"

"It's where we hang out," I said. "If you ain't got anywhere else to go."

But I was already wishing I hadn't said it.

Because it was Friday, and Manny was probably already down there.

Manny was already down there.

"You never answered about how I got this out," Roth says. He's got a twitchy nose. He's the kind of guy you always did figure fucks cats. Who wouldn't even have the decency to duct tape it so it doesn't explode. That kind of guy.

"Walk, motherfucker," I say. "Just fucking walk."

We do, down the alley. Huddled down in our coats, the alley slick and greasy with garbage ice.

And then we stop.

It's Manny. And he ain't moving. He's down on his knees with his head pressed against the asphalt, like listening for a train.

"Fuck you, Roth," I say. "You ain't fucking with me no more."

"This ain't me," Roth says.

"Horseshit." I walk up on Manny, kick him in the ass. "Move, motherfucker."

He doesn't move.

I walk around him.

The profile of his face is pillowed in gore. All the muscles in my body run like water. "You ain't fucking with me?" I say.

"I ain't fucking with you."

I take Manny under the arms, stand to lift him. His body lifts easily, but sticks at the head, stuck on the ground like it's been nailed there. I let him drop, squat down.

"I wouldn't fuck with you," Roth says. "Not like this."

I pull out my Case knife, use it to dig at the frozen blood gluing Manny's skull to the asphalt. Once I've cut free what I can, I take him under his arms again and heave. It's like trying to pull up a railroad tie with your bare hands.

"He's fucked up, for sure," Roth says.

My back bows, my arms grind in my shoulder sockets. I huff and puff, and with a rip his head jerks free, and I tumble heels up backward in the street. Manny flopping over me, his head banging into mine.

"Motherfucker," I say. I'd pulled the skin clean off the left side of his face. Patches of muscle stringing off the bone, an oily discharge where his eye used to be. "Motherfucker," I say again.

"I told you it wasn't me," Roth says.

Then we both stop talking.

Because just barely, but without a doubt, he's breathing. A swirl of breath from the hole in his cheek.

And then there's a laugh from the shadows by the wall.

Eli.

Eli laughing.

But I can't see her laughing. I can't see nothing but her eyes under that hood. That and the hammer in her hand, frosted with blood.

And so I start to laugh too. And so does Roth.

It's those motherfuckers in Toon Town. They don't walk like you and me, they don't exist. Even watching their breath frost through a hole in their cheek with their face ripped half off, they ain't real. See, when you trip on acid, you learn somebody, but you can't learn them motherfuckers. You can't even figure what kind of full of shit they are, whether they fuck cats or don't.

But then you look up at the thin river of sky through the alley buildings, the stars skimming like water bugs, and you think it ain't like that at all. That they're the same kind as you and me, after all. That it's all heartbreak, and there's no deviation from that. Not ever. Your heart will always break for everything that's lost, and what's always lost is everything, and everybody's heart breaks in the exact same way.

But that's horseshit too.

AIRPORT PAPERBACK

ADAM HIRSCH

D ear Maria,
     THANK YOU. I received your ▊▊▊▊ ▊▊▊▊▊▊▊▊▊▊▊▊▊▊▊▊▊▊▊▊▊▊▊▊▊ and the rest. One of the brighter parts of the day-to-day routine is ▊▊▊▊▊▊▊▊▊▊▊▊▊▊▊▊▊ surprisingly modern buildings ▊▊▊▊▊▊▊▊▊▊▊▊▊▊▊▊ so ▊▊▊▊▊▊▊▊▊▊ ▊▊▊▊▊▊▊▊▊▊▊ ▊▊▊▊▊▊▊▊▊▊ ▊▊▊▊▊▊ ▊▊▊▊ ▊▊▊▊▊▊ when it gets cold, the sky fades to the color of concrete. The times we're allowed to roam the camp, I can hear the staccato harmonies of some birds out in the woods. Last week I thought I recognized the song of a ▊▊▊▊▊▊▊.

    And, yes, to answer your question, ▊▊▊▊▊▊

██████████████████████████ We eat. My hair's going; waking up I see more and more thin black strands laying on my pillow. Back in Los Angeles, ████████████████████████████ ████████████████████ ████████ ████████████ █████████ Without question, ██████████████████████ ████████████████████████ an airport paperback, myself in the surreal ████████ █████████ ████████████████████████ I have read it again and again, ████████ the days with bodega stoop ennui, ████████ ████████████████ ████████ but the one thing that has become certain is that I am now a criminal.

████████████████████████ ████████████████████████ for there has always been a Machine and this Machine has monstrously seduced the naïve with promises of wealth and comfort. And they are torn, limb from limb, soul from body, person from community.

I did what I had to, Maria.

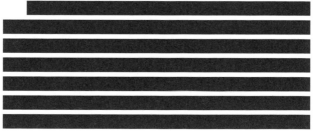

███████████████████████████████ yet ever since, each movement has failed us. The artists have failed us. The intellectuals have failed us. The institutions have failed us. Most of all, the government has failed us.

Let me explain.

I cannot know how or if my letters are ██████, but I want to at ██████████████████████████████.
I was about to fly back to █████████████ after speaking at the ██████████████ Conference in Boston. I remember that morning I was shaving in my room at the Hyatt in Cambridge, hot water steaming up from the sink. I looked in the mirror. I saw a tall man who took care of himself, strong, with thick black hair and the same olive skin of his grandfather, and the same gray eyes his mother had stared down the hate and abuse of her sonofabitch husband, ████████████████████. You know about him.

I looked in the mirror, Maria, and I thought ████████████████████████.

But this was ██████████████████████ in New England. Snow and ice pounded the city. The phone by the bed rang. Wiped the lines of shaving cream from my jaw and ears with a towel and I picked up the phone. ███████████████████████████████
███████████████████████████.

See, I was in the mood ██████████████████
███████████████████████████████

all of whom fashioned themselves as capital-A Artists ██████████████████████████ ██████████████████████████ not writers or painters or ████████████████ or makers or doers, but capital-A Artists. ████████████ sub ██ the Massachusetts weather ██████████████████ I rang up my guy DeRozan ██████████████ who lived in town. Hadn't seen him for years. (Know what, you met him after the mid-term elections, went by Rose. Big guy, muscles, button nose, a sweetheart. Taught █████████████████████████████. Brilliant man, but he smelled like Tide detergent and Drakkar Noir. Remember?) Rose came and picked me up and he and I ██████████████████████████████cheap red wine from coffee mugs████████████████████████████████ ██████████████████████████████

Herbie Hancock, rolling spliffs and he showed me his piece, a nickel plated .45 from his friend.

By ███████████████ we realized we'd lost track of time and needed to get moving ██████████████ █████████████ the ice coming down on the roads. Rose and I walked ████████████████████.

Between the weed and the ██████████████ ████████████████│███████████████████ ████████████████████████████ chicken biryani, ██ ████████████████████████████████████.

it happened. The manager, a short man with glasses, had a humorless demeanor. I stayed at the door. Rose spoke to him. They were talking when the power went out. ████████████████████████████████████ the woman had tears in her eyes, gripping the parka she had on over her sari. We pushed past her and ran out.

The money went to where it was needed.

It was an act of love. And love is only courage in the face of death. That a death, ███████████, may result from my actions is not judgment for the robbery help ███████████████████████████████████. ███████████ people, allegedly injured, but that my book, my crime, will reach many more. ███████████ responding to it? ███████████

You do what you can no matter the secrets or the pain, for to think is the sweetest illegality. I believe it is worth holding out against certain persuasive eventualities. History may give context ██████████████████████████ (Il Grido del Popolo, right?) ███████████████████████████████ ████████████████████████████████████ ████████████████████████████████████ ████████████████████

for human unhappiness is evidence of our own mortality, and █████████████████████████ ████████████████████████████████████ ███████████████████████ justified deportations, ████████████████████████████████████

█████████████████████████████████

█████████████████████████ because what good is
theory in the face of survival? The one thing that is
certain is that I am a criminal.

I have to wrap it up now. I am tired. My hand
aches. Tell ██████████ I miss him, and to strong
█████████████████████████████████

and I can't ████████ ████████ because I don't
█████████████████████████████ So please
tell him ██████████████████████████████,
please, Maria; please tell him that with all my heart I
████████.

Love,
Julian Esparza

A BEAD TO STRING

MICHAEL HARRIS COHEN

What do you want to hear? Should I tell you about the flowers? How they bloomed like jewels until weeds choked them. Should I tell you why weeds are superior to flowers? They're a more honest marker. Especially in her case, on her grave, which I dug with bare hands. Yes, note that down. I want it remembered. You see, flowers try too hard. Egoists of the plant world, I never liked them. Neither did she. We had that in common. At least that. She was a woman of unusual tastes but I suppose that's obvious. I could tell you too how she never liked handsome men. "Too easy to admire," she said. "Ugly men try harder." Like the weeds I suppose. Flowers need tending. They're fussy and delicate. Weeds simply grow. They take over everything. Funny. I never made the connection before. It's the geometry of thought I suppose.

When you leave this room you'll pin a photo to a wall, draw a line to another photo, maybe affix a Post-it next to the line. Isn't that how you do it? That's how they do it on TV. Lines and photos and notes, then they step back for the big picture, take it all in, uncover the connection that eluded them. Things come together in ways we never imagined. As a child I never imagined I'd be capable of doing what I've done. I had pets and loved them. Did you imagine you'd be doing what you do? Did you imagine you'd be poring over pictures of skinned bodies? Or limbless ones? Did you imagine you'd spend your life with the dead instead of the living?

The dead govern you. They summon you from bed in the middle of the night. They implore you to learn their secrets though they have none. They got their ticket punched, that's all. Of course, even if you catch the one who punched the ticket—that dark train conductor—you never understand him. Not really. Sure, you grasp the henpecked man who shotguns his wife's head onto the wall; the battered woman who's had enough and immolates her husband in his bed. Those are easy "whys." It's the others that nag: the loving father, dressed in his perfect life, who returns from the office and drowns his six-year-old in the tub. Prom queen suicides and high school massacres. Those linger. Those inscrutabilities live in your gut. They own you, the dead and their killers. They set the course of your life. They know what you will never know. If we're honest—we need to be honest, right?—you're the caboose and I'm the engineer. We're joined but you'll never reach me. It's not ego or bluster. It's fact.

Still, I never imagined I'd be here. A failure of my imagination, perhaps, or plain old hubris. I never imagined this interview. Or is that the wrong word? "Evaluation"? "Interrogation"? How could we see this moment before it arrived. Which string of our life led us toward this?

You must be exhausted. You look it. That's your fourth coffee. I feel like I've lived and died a dozen times in this room. Though for me it's easier. I just talk and talk. But you have to parse my words, try to fish out what lies beneath. You want reasons. Motive. History. Not just a cop, a shrink-cop. Shrink-wrapped, enfolded in a jaded and broken human. A cop draws the lines and connects the dots. His evidence is at least things he can see and touch and smell. Not you. You chase what cannot be seen or fixed. You chase the unknowable. Knock at the impenetrable. Might as well try to understand what a bird thinks when it hits a window. There's something between us. Can't you see it? You're smashing your beak on it.

You fidget with your pen, take notes, act empathetic, hope for something new to be revealed, one more fact, a bead to string, to close the circle, to lead you back to "why." Of course you know behind every why is another, doors that stretch back to the dawn of man, and have you ever considered that if man has a dawn doesn't it stand to reason he also has a dusk? I think about these things.

I don't want to bore you. I know what you want. You want novelty or a crescendo. What if I told you there were others, that she was not the first but just another bead on *my* string? What if I told you she was not even the last? Did you know if you're well dressed and white, and drive the right car, you can knock on almost any door in this state? You just look through their mail, then you put on a tie and go right up to that door and knock. When they open, you put on your biggest smile, the one without a drop of hate or guile in it. You clench it on, though it hurts your face, you reach out your hand and speak the name you just learned: "Jim (or John or Roger or Sarah), goddamn it's been a *long* time. How the hell are ya? I was in the neighborhood and . . ." They're more afraid of embarrassing themselves for not remembering than of inviting you inside. And once you're inside, you're in.

Would it help if I told you that humans are a mistake? Or would you rather hear that her last breath, the last breath of all of them, sounded like the start of a story and not the end? I don't mean to be obtuse. If I could explain, if I could turn my skull inside out for you, believe me I would. But we're stuck in this

86

moment. Me on one side of the table, you on the other. Both handcuffed. You just can't see yours. I see them, though. Clear as the moon. This table between us, it might as well be an ocean, swelling larger by the second. That's how it is. That's how it always is. And there's not a question or an answer or a why that will ever span the distance.

THE FIFTH OF JULY

HELEN PHILLIPS

We were sitting on folding chairs in an empty field behind a gas station to watch the county fireworks from afar. Recently one of us had almost died.

"Hecho en México," the broken Coca-Cola bottle bragged.

Cigarette butts, sagebrush, bottle caps, the usual decorations.

Among us four siblings we'd killed five (maybe seven) prairie dogs with a BB gun that day. Pest control. Local recreation.

We sat in a row, four folding chairs of different colors and heights, waiting for the fireworks to start. It seemed they should have started by now. Under other circumstances there would have been a kid here, a kid or two, a bit of progeny, a niece or a nephew, but there were no kids.

We speculated about where those prairie dogs were now. What was going on with their carcasses. Like, were they lying there stiff in the tunnels below us with their little arms flung above their heads?

One of us went inside to ask the guy in the gas station if he could maybe turn off the neon sign so there would be more darkness. He was a nice guy. His wife and kids were there to say hi on their way into town, where they were going to lie on blankets in the plaza and really see the fireworks. He seemed to have two sets of twins, if that's possible—a pair of little boys and a pair of slightly bigger girls. Those kids! They had such clean, dark hair. He said he was sorry he couldn't turn the sign off; maybe we should go into the plaza too? He had to work but his wife could drive in front of us and show us the exact way. It was no use explaining that the plaza (crowds, germs) wasn't an option for us.

All day we'd been driving around, looking for something, but we just kept passing the parking lot where the garbage trucks were parked. We couldn't believe how many garbage trucks there were for such a small municipality. On the opposite side of town we passed a souvenir shop with the most enormous amethyst geode in the window. As though the garbage trucks were balancing one side of the scale and the geode the other.

"The four of you should go away together somewhere for a few days. Boost each other up after all this. What are siblings for anyway. Be carefree. You've earned it."

We'd spent the whole day craving sopaipillas, but we hadn't been able to find them anywhere. All we found was this hippie selling a garment he alleged could be made into forty-one different garments.

"Loaves and fishes," he kept saying, "loaves and fishes."

Right when the fireworks started a man in a cowboy hat came around the side of the gas station. We were scared until he stuck out his hand and went down the row and introduced himself as Jack Flores, the fellow running for coroner. He said he was en route to the plaza. He said he was responsible for a quarter of the fireworks and he hoped we enjoyed them. We told him we'd seen his campaign billboard. "Billboards," he corrected. We didn't tell him we weren't from around here and had no dog in his fight. We didn't tell him his campaign billboard scared us. That way he was smiling, as though he was trying to hide something in his mouth. We hadn't even realized that coroners could be elected officials. It didn't work that way where we were from, or maybe it did and we were just ignorant. "Lot of prairie dogs in this field," Jack Flores informed us, gazing at one that had just popped up. "They carry bubonic plague, you know," he said. "That's the kind of thing we could try to, you know, take care of. Change somehow."

"Thanks," we said, not certain what we were thanking him for. But we were glad he wouldn't mind about the killed prairie dogs. We weren't sure what you call a coroner—Mr. or Dr.?

We asked Jack Flores where we could get sopaipillas. He listed four places right off the bat and then asked for our phone number, he could have his secretary call us with more information. Just then it occurred to him that if we didn't know where sopaipillas could be acquired we must be out-of-towners with no dog in his fight, and he was already rushing off by the time one of us came up with the final digits of a fake phone number. We looked up at the fireworks.

Dogs alerted their masters to the end of the world. Their masters ignored them, went outside to stand beneath colored bombs.

"I used to be scared of those, you know, skeleton ladies driving the wooden carts, but now I really want one. We have to buy one before we leave, okay."

During the fireworks a feeling of threat arose. Was it prairie dogs or dogs or La Muerte in her cart? Whose red eyes surveyed the napes of our necks?

We were scared but also we were bored, already numb to the fireworks.

We were bored but mainly we were fragile. You think a brush with death is an inoculation against death?

When we were children all four of us would try to squeeze into one twin bed. Someone always fell out but still it was a sort of comfort. In the morning our parents made fun of us for needing each other so much.

○

Were the prairie dogs going to attack us or not?

Was anything they did to us a legitimate expression of grief? The same desire for revenge we would have if the situations were reversed?

Twenty-four hours from now we'll be sitting in a cracked hot tub, drinking beers, gazing at a row of beer cans holed by BB guns. The scars from May, witnessed for the first time, our eyes looking and not looking. By then we'll have done the thing we were bound to do, the thing in the parking lot, the woman in the rear-view mirror, her gestures of confusion, a dent in her parked car created by the back of our car, our apparent indifference as we drove too quickly away. But we were not indifferent. Leftover fireworks going off all around town. Extravagant trash along the highway, a piece of blue-and-white cake on a red plastic plate. July Fifth.

"Will these fireworks never end?" we asked one another on July Fourth.

The prairie dogs stood in the field staring upward like prophets.

WITHHOLD THE DAWN

RICHIE NARVAEZ

Gladys Gutierrez hated the IRS. In her mind, the IRS had destroyed her parents, crossing them out of her existence like disallowed itemized deductions. It didn't matter to her that Mami and Papi had neglected to pay taxes for a dozen years apiece, Gladys still wanted revenge. From dawn to dusk and even in her dreams.

To that end, she purchased—*on sale!*—a thirty-two-inch Summerfield Tru-Cut™ axe, drop-forged of carbon steel with an American hickory handle. "Summerfield," the slogan went. "When you want something *chop chop!*"

She never dated, never married, never held an honest job. Revenge was her only companion. Each year she moved to a new town, created a new identity, sent in new tax returns. She bungled the numbers on purpose, giving herself exceedingly generous refunds. Most times, she got the money. This disappointed her. While she enjoyed the cash, the reward she craved was that neat letter in a neat envelope from the IRS. There would be an audit. An agent would be coming by.

In Wyoming, for example, Gladys claimed she worked as a safari guide. Two months later, an IRS agent named Steven W. Cabeza-Plana rang her doorbell.

"Miss Theodora Ratatouille?"

"*C'est moi,*" said Gladys.

Cabeza-Plana's hair was stuccoed in place. His teeth were bathroom tiles. Gladys disliked him immediately and offered him iced tea.

Cabeza-Plana said, "Aces," and asked her for her receipts. He sat down, removing neat papers from his briefcase and flicking his pen. Gladys went to her bedroom, pretending to look for receipts. But in reality, she sat on her bed and quietly sang Don McLean's "American Pie." Using the axe as a microphone.

In the eight minutes and thirty-three seconds it took to finish all the verses, the anesthetic in the tea would kick in. Gladys emerged from her bedroom, twirling her beloved Summerfield axe and half-murmuring, "February made me shiver / With every paper I'd deliver."

Numb and paralyzed but still awake, Cabeza-Plana listened as she hacked off his right arm, then his left.

"Drove my Chevy to the levee but the levee was dry."

Then, as was her habit, she made agent meat loaf, empanadas, and guisada. She ate like a one-percenter for days.

But, over time, Gladys found she had less luck. Year after year, refund after refund arrived without question. She became rich. But she ached with an awful hankering. And her Summerfield rusted with ennui.

So when she moved to Klamath Falls, she sent out ten different forms using twelve different names. Sure enough, neat little letters started arriving in the mail.

Four agents came by in one week, all carrying neat briefcases and flicking pens. The first one did not drink enough tea, so when Gladys emerged with her Summerfield, a scuffle seemed about to ensue. But the agent had spilled the tea on the floor and, approaching Gladys in his wingtips, had slipped, tripping and sending his forehead right into the edge of her axe. With the second and third agents, everything went hunky-dory. Tea. "Pie." Chop. In fact, by the time the fourth agent arrived, Gladys found herself bored. She brought the axe to the door and took him out just as he stepped in. Then she did yoga.

That month, Gladys made so much meat loaf, empanadas, and guisada that she began selling the extra. Everyone on the block said they were delish. She was even written up in a neighbor's blog, something that delighted her because who wouldn't want to be on a blog?

It also made her wonder if perhaps the ardor of her revenge had been quelled. Yes, perhaps it was time to put away her faithful Summerfield and have a real life, to sleep next to something warm and soft, not cold and sharp.

And then one day, in hazy August, the doorbell rang.

"Mrs. Feldshuh, my name is Chris Haragán, and I'm from the IRS."

Slouching and unzipped, Haragán did not seem at all like an IRS agent to Gladys.

"Don't be alarmed, ma'am, I was going to send a letter, but I got busy at work, my grandmother passed, my cat got this weird eye infection. Listen, I'm sorry. Here's the letter. I did type it."

Haragán handed her a dirty envelope. Gladys didn't understand. She had already received her refund under the name Feldshuh. Twice. Gladys took the filthy envelope. The letter inside was wrinkled and a coffee stain made a crude yet artistic design in one corner.

"What's the hullabaloo?" she said.

"I happen to subscribe to your neighbor's blog," said Haragán, "and I read about the success of your home business. Frankly, ma'am, I think you're making money that belongs to the government."

"Would you like some iced tea?" she said.

"No, thanks, ma'am. Do you mind if I smoke?"

"I guess," she said.

Gladys found that she was irresistibly attracted to this fellow. But he was IRS. And she hated the IRS. She could sneak up behind him with her cherished Summerfield—so she wouldn't have to see his pallid, scrambled-egg-speckled face. It would only take one good swing to get through that skinny, razor-burn-lined neck.

Instead she began to cry.

"Mrs. Feldshuh, there, there." Haragán held her.

She would have stopped crying but the smoke from the cigarette hanging in his mouth made her eyes water. And she didn't want him to stop holding her. So she kept crying. And coughing a little.

Eventually, the cigarette went out and Gladys fried some meat loaf slices for both of them. After the meal, he said, "I'd love to try some of that iced tea now."

That set Gladys to crying again. She said, "My name isn't Barbara Ann Feldshuh, and I'm not an Amish electrical engineer."

"Of course not. You're a forest fire lookout."

"Not that either, you silly fool."

And so Gladys confessed to this man with whom she had fallen hopelessly in love by his second helping of meat loaf. Hours later, when she finished, he said: "Really?"

They made love half-on and half-off the kitchen island right then and there.

The next morning Haragán returned, freshly showered and shaved, and smelling lightly of coffee and its aftereffects. He brought three Federal agents and a bouquet of freesia.

The Summerfield axe sang to Gladys from the bedroom, called for her to wield it as the deadly instrument of justice it had been purchased—*on sale!*—to be. She ran toward it. But all three of the agents tased her.

"My boss is so proud of me for this. I hope you know how grateful I am. Oh, and thanks for lunch yesterday," Haragán said, winking.

Although the families of the IRS agents Gladys had killed and cooked with oregano, sofrito, and a teaspoon of cumin almost all forgave her on a highly rated episode of *Good Morning America*, she spent the rest of her life in a penitentiary, sullen and unpardoned.

As for her precious Summerfield—after spending years in a lockup, it was auctioned off, then passed from owner to owner, from year to year, and all the while, from dawn to dusk and even in its dreams, it hummed a Don McLean tune and dreamed of revenge.

GOOD HAIR

MARTA BALCEWICZ

One hair was stuck to the vent in the center of the dashboard. Another lay across the bulbous gear shifter, inscribed with a "V" for Volvo.

We were done.

Jeffrey zipped his pants. We sat in silence for a couple minutes. Then he sat up. "Better get rid of these," he said, and started plucking the hairs—from the vent, volume dial, cup-holder.

I was speechless.

It was his expression. Jeffrey's nose wrinkled and his lips curled, like he was picking gunk off an old sweater. It meant nothing to him that the hairs came off my head, that they were chock-full of DNA belonging to the woman he took to parking lots twice a week.

It could only mean one thing: there was someone else. I mean, someone other than Rose-Lynn, his wife.

The next day I waited outside Jeffrey's office in my brown Honda. When he got into his Volvo, I followed him, down two, three, eight streets, taking turns I knew weren't leading to his house. Twenty minutes later, he pulled into the Oyster Inn, on the beach. Cheap but not unromantic. He stepped out of his car, walked toward a parked older model Jetta in a fun-loving shade of turquoise, and leaned into the open passenger's-side window.

Something was off. It was the color. And the car model. The two combined.

Jeffrey pointed to the check-in office and jogged toward it.

I parked my car, got out, and speed-walked to the Jetta. It was definitely the color. "Fun-loving turquoise." A custom color. Just as I'd described in my novel.

I knocked on the driver's-side window. I saw movement. She was gathering her purse, spitting out gum. Always with her gum. (Paranoid about halitosis. My "humanizing trait." Chapter 2.)

"Yeah?" she said, rolling down the window. Her makeup-model lips bent into a nasty zigzag. She was not a good human being. Not giving. But I knew all this before seeing her expression. Yup, I knew everything. I could've been a single mother with a flat tire (Chapter 4), I could've been running from a mugger

(Chapter 8). Whatever the scenario, she'd refuse to offer assistance, think of herself only, say no, and toss her incredible hair.

The hair.

More than anything, it was the hair that identified her. I've always had a thing for Samson, so I gave my heroine a wonderful mane. Luscious, long, blond— I doled out the adjectives (Chapters 1 through 36). I even named her Samantha—almost Samson.

"Sam?" I said.

"Do I know you?" There it was again. The snarl of a cold, clammed human being (bad childhood, alcoholic mother). From the first to last chapter she stayed that way, collecting victims stupidly snared by her coolness.

"We worked together at the call center," I said. I knew her employment history, naturally.

"Oh, okay," she said. "Listen, I'm kind of busy here."

"No problem. Just wanted to say hey!" I darted away, pointing to the 7-Eleven across the street to explain my hurry.

Sam started rolling up her window. I saw her shake her head. Next she'd mutter an expletive and forget all about me.

I ran back to my car and draped my jacket over my head, leaving a tiny slit for my eyes. I saw Jeffrey return and showily dangle a key with a novelty-sized

Sebastian, the Disney crustacean, attached to it. He and Samantha climbed to a room on the second level and shut the door behind them.

Two hours later they dashed out and hopped over to Frocker's BBQ next door. I watched Sam's hair bounce as she ran. It was like a third entity going out for BBQ with them.

Since Jeffrey was a pig when it came to grilled meat, I had time.

First, I tried the door to their room, but no luck. It was locked.

I went to the check-in office and found a teenager watching a movie on his laptop.

"I'm locked out!" I said helplessly. "Room 202. My boyfriend ran out for food."

The teen was hesitant.

"He took the key," I went on. "It had Sebastian on it."

That seemed to do it. He nodded and looked down at his laptop. "Is your boyfriend Jeffrey Beazel?"

I hid in the walk-in closet. Within an hour the key turned in the lock.

"I need Pepto-Bismol," Jeffrey groaned. A door shut. He'd gone into the bathroom.

From the crack I'd left in the closet door, I had a perfect view of the bed. Sam lay down on it sideways.

Her hair splayed out on the duvet like a golden octopus. She placed one hand over her eyes.

I knew her well.

I knew she didn't want the man in the bathroom ("Never again will I touch venison," Jeffrey said over a watery burp). Heck, I didn't even want him. I mean, after today.

I pushed the door open. It didn't make a creak. I walked toward the bed, quickly. The carpeting muffled my steps. I stood right overtop Sam, casting a shadow on her pretty face. She lifted her hand from her eyes. She saw me. Her eyes widened but not as big as you'd think. She'd seen crazier stuff in her time.

"Shhh." I put my finger over my lips. "I want to get rid of him, too." I pointed to the bathroom door and made a grossed-out expression.

Sam's lip curled. She sat up and I plopped myself on the bed next to her, like we were old friends.

"How much do you owe him?" she asked, and before I could understand, she added, "I'm at twelve thousand. I'll never have that kind of cash."

I nodded. I'd never borrowed a cent from Jeff, but now it all made sense. Sam had always been terrible with money.

"I'm thinking: your hair," I said, picking up a tress and smoothing it in my palm.

Sam looked a little taken aback. Maybe I was being too familiar.

"To strangle him," I explained.

"Oh." Her face softened. She understood and cracked up a bit, like I'd made a good joke. Then she went serious and shook her head. She reached for her purse, lying on the floor next to the bed, and opened it. Inside, nestled into the silky lining, was a gun, petite and elegant, just like my protagonist.

"Of course," I said. I felt like an idiot for tabling the hair idea. (Jeffrey started gurgling water, making dumb walrus sounds.) "I was joking about the hair," I explained, waving my hand and checking her perfect face for signs of disapproval. But Sam's thoughts were elsewhere—obviously. She was already pushing me back into the closet. The cool woman, the cooler woman, the more beautiful one certainly. It was no wonder Jeffrey had moved on to her, a blonde with a tiny pistol.

Sam shut the door behind me. "Good luck!" I squeaked. But she didn't respond. I sat on the floor, next to a fallen hanger. Even though I knew something big was about to happen all I could think about was what Sam and I might do after. I mean, after-after—after we'd disposed of the body. What we'd do tomorrow.

DOGFACE

SARAH WANG

L et's call Dogface," Elma called up from the bottom bunk. "It's the first of the month."

Dogface had been mauled by a dog as a child, and time labored tirelessly to stretch and deepen the long, pulpy scars on the left side of his face. His bargain-bin weed was full of seeds that crackled and popped, and it always came flat, as if it had been pressed between the pages of a heavy book. Surely he would be in high spirits tonight. It was payday from the government. Can you be on disability for having a mangled face, we wondered? What other parts of his body had been unspeakably mangled on that fateful dog day? On the first of the month Dogface bought us atomic nachos, which he watched us eat while smoking rocks of crack cocaine on the other end of the couch, our fingers dripping with what resembled melted yellow plastic.

"Bowling alley." Magda swung down from the top bunk after hanging up the phone. "Show starts at nine."

At the former bowling alley that now functioned as a venue for bands to play, we circled around with our gazes fixed somewhere in the distance. We never looked directly at anyone. If we happened to catch someone's eye, we always looked away immediately in exasperation. We perched on a long lunch counter near the door, sipping on a shared waxed paper cup of Suicide. That's what we called it, all the sodas from the fountain mixed together. Kids rolled heavy balls at each other, scuttling out of the way to avoid being hit, sneakers squealing across the dull wood floor. The grumble of balls rolling evoked the ghostly noise of pins clattering and toppling, though it had been years since the bowling alley had been functional. The seventies were still alive here, mainly in the form of the orange, yellow, and green squirts painted on the walls, and the lacquered mustard tabletops that teenagers splayed upon.

Magda's cousin was about to come on. His band dragged their equipment down the lanes and began setting up. The bass player stepped into the gutter and fell, smashing his guitar on the hardwood floor.

"Ha-ha," someone yelled. The sound traveled

down the lanes, and three seconds later, Magda's cousin looked up and threw a middle finger in the direction of the crowd. The "ha-ha" had come from Dogface's mouth. Only half of his face was animate, leering in satisfaction, while the other half was set in a permanent half-stunned, half-semiconscious expression by scar tissue. Most people were terrified of him, but he had drugs and could buy beer, so we remained complicit in the collective denial of our own terror. He exhaled a billow of smoke and flicked his cigarette, still burning, into the middle of a bowling lane.

Magda grabbed me and I reached to yank Elma, who was so busy looking nowhere that she didn't see me waving three inches from her face.

"Sup?" Dogface nodded. He shoved his hand into the pocket of his giant army jacket.

"Sup?" we replied, one echo in three different pitches.

"Sup?" he said again. Dogface had the jaw of a pit bull and the brains of a chicken.

"Got a lil' sack for us?" Elma asked, crossing her arms over her baggy shirt.

"Nope." He pulled out a bindle from his pocket. "Got this though."

"I'm not smoking crack. Once was enough," Magda said. "The last time I did drugs with you, you stayed up for three days with a shotgun propped in your lap peering out of the blinds. Dark, dude."

109

"This isn't crack. It's mescaline."

"What's mescaline?" I asked.

"It's from peyote." Elma's eyes widened. "I've always wanted to have a psychedelic spiritual communion on peyote."

Dogface opened the paper bindle and shook four tiny maroon pills into his palm. Elma looked at me. I shrugged, raising one eyebrow. She grabbed a pill and sucked it up.

"Waaaaait a minute," Magda said, sighing. "What's that gonna do to you?"

"Trip you the fuck out." Dogface smiled. He took one and ate it.

"Uh-uh." Magda shook her head. "No way."

Dogface lifted his palm up to me, as if he wanted me to lick a pill out of his hand. I took one and pretended to pop it in my mouth. The band started playing; we snaked to the front. Magda's cousin couldn't play any instruments, but he was an enthusiastic dancer. He sang, at first sliding around stiffly tethered by the mic cord, and then breaking out of his own body like he was undead. The drummer smashed behind him coolly, looking around the bowling alley as if he had no interest at all in what his body was doing.

Magda hopped around on one foot until she couldn't balance anymore before switching to the other. "Are you tripping yet?" she asked me.

I shook my head, holding the pinched pill up for

her to see as the band started a new song. After the band finished playing, I sold the pill for twenty bucks to a girl wearing a clear plastic raincoat in the parking lot next to the neighboring pupuseria's dumpsters.

Outside, Magda stole a beer from some guy's backpack. She stood behind him and opened the zipper slowly while I chatted him up. We darted away giggling, leaving him with his backpack gaping. Asshole. Around the corner at the taco truck, we ate five tacos each, courtesy of my recent drug deal, before waddling back to the parking lot. Where was Elma? The last time we saw her she and Dogface were tiptoeing around the bowling alley alternately bug eyed and giggly, communicating with one another through rapid blinking. They smelled the holes in the bowling balls while wearing their shoes on the wrong feet because, Elma attested, it felt correct.

Magda shotgunned the beer while I scanned the parking lot. We weaved between cars, stopping to pop a squat while the other looked out. There she was. Elma sitting in my Beetle in a dark spot behind the bowling alley. I ran over while Magda was still in mid-pee, leaving her pulling up her pants and shouting angrily after me. Knocking on the window, I mimed for Elma to unlock the door. She stared down, unmoving.

"Can she even hear right now?" Magda arrived, wiping her hands on her pants.

I knocked on the window again. "EL-MA. EL-MA."

"Don't you have a key? This is your car, isn't it?" Magda said.

"Oh yeah." I unlocked the door.

"Is this what a spiritual communion looks like?" Magda asked.

Elma was so out of it she kept stretching her cheeks with both hands while staring at her feet. After shaking her and making sure she was breathing right, we decided to take her home immediately.

Magda climbed into the back on the driver's side. I started the engine, which came to life choking and gasping, grabbing on to this side of the world with a tenuous grip.

"What's up, ladies?"

It was Magda's cousin.

"We're leaving, that's what's up. Ciao." Magda waved.

I put the Beetle in reverse.

"Uh, I wouldn't do that if I were you," the drummer said.

"What, why?" I asked. I pointed at Elma. "She burned."

"You're gonna slice his wiener off, that's what," he said, peering inside.

I looked down at Elma's feet. A Harley mat covering a hole that had rusted through the floorboard was gone. Sticking up from the hole was an erect penis, glowing faintly in the dark. It was Dogface, lying on his back, propped up underneath the Beetle holding his boner up through the rusty hole. It stuck straight up into the car, like a tumescent sapling.

"This is some sick perv shit," Magda said from the backseat. "Get him out of there."

"I can't just pull him out," Magda's cousin said. "His wiener is totally, uh engaged." He made a chopping motion with one arm.

By this time, a small group had flocked around us. I wanted to drag Dogface out by his legs. I didn't care if his penis was lopped off. Magda protested. We had to withdraw his boner first to get him out, she reasoned. I was losing patience. I reached over Elma, through the open window, grabbed the drummer's beer out of his hand, and poured it in the hole over Dogface's penis.

The crowd clapped as his dick, Magda proudly announced, wilted.

SEE AGENT

ANONYMOUS

The agent starts the feed again.

The nun slides her card through the cloven slot, waiting for it to click and say GO, but the turnstile gives her a bad read. She swipes again and again, infinite times, but the turnstile whines and repeats, PLEASE SWIPE AGAIN. Soon, her arm's cramping and she can hear a train. When she tries a quicker swipe, her cowl wags and the turnstile says, TOO FAST SWIPE SLOWER. In response, she slides her card through at a sarcastic pace, and the turnstile replies, TOO SLOW SWIPE FASTER.

Everyone has a breaking point, even nuns. The small green caps on the rectangular panel remind her of old computers. Obviously the fare hikes aren't going toward turnstiles. She whispers a prayer to

St. Christopher, and swipes once more, smoothly, perfectly, and in response the turnstile says, JUST USED.

"Liar," the nun hisses.

The agent always enjoys this part when she bites her fist.

Now the nun has to wait eighteen minutes before
she can use her card again. She has no spare change
and a carpal twinge in her swipe arm. She fingers her
beads, takes a deep breath, and swipes once more.
This time, the turnstile makes a high-pitched sigh
she's never heard one make before and says, SEE AGENT.
The glass cube where the subway attendants normally
sit—like penitents atoning for sin—is empty. "There
is no agent," says the nun. The sound of her own voice
echoing through the station startles her. A dormant
MetroCard vending machine leers from a wall.

It is two in the morning. She has come from the
hospital, having been summoned to perform the Last
Sacrament over a dying man. "Only say the word, sister," said the dying man, "and I shall return home."
When the man finally closed his eyes, so too in tired-
ness did the nun. "May our brother safely reach your
kingdom," said the nun. She sat by his bed, ignored
by the grieving wife. Hours later the soft flatline of the
monitor woke her to the sight of the new widow staring
silently at the still body.

A distant thrum and clang grows louder as the train
approaches. The deserted platform seems near enough
for her to touch. A nun lives by God's law, but also

abides the laws of man. She has no fealty to the laws of machines. She would never hop a turnstile without paying, but she has paid, and the turnstile is holding her hostage for more money. It feels unkind, perhaps even like a sin, one which, in a strange new compartment of her heart, she hopes God will punish.

"Have you no shame?" says the nun.

A whispery glitch-like beep leaks from the turnstile, then a sound at a strangely lower pitch. The note bends, sinking lower, until it fades completely.

She hasn't even swiped.

HE SEES, says the turnstile.

The nun squints at the letters on the display to make sure she isn't having a vision. She isn't. It says, HE SEES.

"Who sees?" asks the nun.

THE AGENT, says the turnstile.

The headlights of the train begin to brighten the station. There are no agents. There are no anyones. There are only malfunctioning machines that know naught of human guilt or grief or love or death or sleep. Were the agent here, he would take pity and allow her through.

"Lord, help me," she says, hoisting herself off the ground on trembling arms.

YOU WILL PAY, says the turnstile.

Sweat beads instantly at her hairline as she tries once, twice to swing herself clear. On the third try, however, her elbows buckle mid-swing and her legs tangle in the three-limbed pivot. The nun spills over the turnstile and lands headfirst on the other side. *The agent can't stop laughing.* Before passing out, she watches the train float sideways into the station from where she rests on the filthy platform. *The agent is laughing so hard.* A lone rat shakes its head from the warning tread, then disappears onto the tracks. *The agent is laughing so hard he is blind with tears.* Dreamlike relief settles over her when the train stops, its headlights bending and breaking against the tiles, filling the station with a million glowing eyes.

THESE ARE FUNNY, BROKEN DAYS

AMBER SPARKS

I have two knives.

By that I mean I have one knife plus Dave who also has a knife.

God, that's funny. It's funny, right? I think it's funny.

Do you remember that actor? The one with the squint and the blond hair? Used to be big? Pretty? Kind of goofy? Smokes like a European? That's how Dave looks. Women like him. Even without little toes. We pair well that way. Women, men, they like us both. Both like us both.

But Dave, he has these qualms. Morals-ish. I,

119

though, am a spear tip and I contain no morals. Why bother? I don't waste time agonizing over things. Sure, there's something wrong with me. But I can't change the way I am. Not that I don't enjoy it. I do. I wouldn't do it if I did not. But it's actually very hard. Everyone thinks it would be easy, but no, no it is not. You have to work really hard at it, like a job. Skin and teeth and nails are tough. Blood smells bad. Not everything burns.

It has to be worth it.

Dave loves me but feels the danger of me like his hairs are constantly standing at attention. Prickly for me, that's what he says. He only goes for helpless young blondes, drunk at campus bars. They're bleached and empty and nothing at all like me. I suppose that's why he likes me, why he hates me.

Sometimes, after I get done with a john, I tell Dave he's next. That while he's sleeping I'm going to stick him, right between the ribs. He gets really scared then, doesn't sleep, just stares at my hands for hours and days. Once he cried.

Isn't that funny? Funny ha-ha, I mean. Seriously. A knife afraid of a knife.

These are funny, broken days. We fit right in.

LOOPHOLE

ADAM STERNBERGH

He understands what's coming next. He feels like he's been here before.

These blank walls, this bare table. A black woman in a white lab coat, watching. Her hair cut short and dyed blond. Clipboard poised.

On the table, a button.

On the wall, a speaker.

He sits patiently.

Waiting for the prompt.

There's nothing on the clipboard. It's just a prop, for show. She pretends to read her empty page, then watches him over the clipboard.

This kind of scenario is illegal. Or, at least, the kind of scenario that the subject believes he is participating in is illegal.

This scenario is not actually illegal.

Not yet.

He doesn't think he'll press it. He'll hear a voice, garbled, he knows, over the speaker. The other person, answering a question. If the answer is wrong, they'll prompt him.

The answer will be wrong.

He knows that, too.

Then he'll press the button.

Or not.

A small jolt. That's what they told him.

Just a little bit of pain.

Then more pain. Each time he presses.

If he presses.

That's up to him.

She studied the Milgram experiment in school. Conducted back in the 1940s, over a hundred years ago. In which subjects were prodded to administer painful jolts to an anonymous unseen recipient in another room. Jolts of increasing intensity. There was no recipient in those experiments. The screams were just an actor. It was a hoax, to see if people would do it.

They did it.

That kind of experiment is not legal anymore.

This experiment is legal, technically, though she understands they're bending the rules a bit.

He can't see the other person, of course. The other person is seated in another room, hidden from view. The other person can't see him either, so the other person will never know who pressed the button that caused the pain.

If he presses. Which he doesn't think he will.

He's not a monster, after all.

He's not required to press it. He knows this because, many years ago, he was the other person in an experiment like this one, on the other side of the jolts.

And whoever it was in the other room pressed the button.

Again and again.

He was just a young man then, desperate for cash. Willing to be a guinea pig.

Now he's a middle-aged man, desperate for cash.

But I'll only do it this time if I get to be the one with the button, he told them.

To his surprise, they agreed.

O

Another thing she studied in graduate school was a history of the theories of time. For many years, the popular conception of time was that it was much like a river. You are stationary. Time passes. Events happen in a discernible sequence: past, present, future. To move extemporaneously, out of time, to travel in time, would be like stepping out of the river and then stepping back in, upstream or downstream. This seemed to be theoretically possible. In hindsight, it's clear why they were never able to practically conquer the problem.

The other person's voice will be electronically garbled beyond all comprehension. The other person is a paid volunteer, looking for an easy hundred dollars, just like him.

You'll get used to the pain, he wants to tell the other person. It will make you angry, sure. It will make you question what kind of monster sits in another room and doles out excruciating jolts to a stranger.

But it will fade. The pain.

What else lingers, he's not qualified to say.

Did it affect him? Sure. He was young then. Twenty years ago, at least. The following decades haven't been kind. Regrets? Definitely. Mistakes? Of course. Jail? Take a guess.

After all, if he'd made the right choices, he wouldn't be back here.

So, yes, it left him angry. It changed him in some way. Taught him what people are capable of.

His finger inches toward the button.

Isn't that a lesson this other person might also want to learn?

The theory of time in which she had been trained was much different from the river metaphor. Quantum physics had revealed to them the reality of time. There is no past, present, or future, no causality, no consequence, no progress. Time is not a succession of moments. It is more like an infinite number of moments occurring simultaneously. Your experience of time as happening in sequence is simply a trick of human perception. You are like a rider in a train, passing a series of billboards. These billboards are every moment in your life. To you, these moments seem to happen in sequence. But to the outside observer, they exist simultaneously and you are the one who is moving.

Think of it like a filmstrip, her professor told her. (Tells her.) A filmstrip is simply a series of images, all of which exist. But when you run the strip through a projector, it looks like sequence. It looks like life.

She nodded. (Nods.)

And once we understand this, he explained (is explaining), time travel is no longer the challenge. The challenge is to see if, by bending the filmstrip, by breaching time, the events of one moment can be made to alter the nature of another simultaneous moment.

If these moments can interact.

He shifts in his chair.

He remembers the electrodes. That they used a special jelly to attach them.

To increase the conductivity.

She startles when the garbled voice comes over the speaker.

He looks to the woman to confirm that they've begun.

She nods.

The other person gets the answer wrong.

A red light lights.

He hits the button.

Thinking about it later, he'll realize he didn't even hesitate.

She wishes she could be in that other room. She wishes she could watch that other person. She wonders if the two of them look alike. Well, of course they do, she thinks.

She is receiving her diploma with honors from graduate school right now.

She is breaking up with her high school boyfriend right now.

She is painstakingly picking out the gum that a girl threw into her large halo of curly hair on the first day of second grade right now.

She is getting news that her brother in the service died overseas right now.

She is cutting her hair short and dyeing it blond right now.

She is standing in the room with the clipboard right now.

He is being offered a hundred dollars right now.

He is being asked the impossible question right now.

A factory is manufacturing the special jelly right now, and packing it into a box, and loading it into a truck.

Right now.

All moments are happening simultaneously, always.

The trick is to see if you can bring two such moments into proximity.

So that one will affect the other.

The other person, on the other side of the speaker, calls out, more in surprise than pain.

Get ready, he thinks. Because it only gets worse.

He hits the button again.

He feels the pain again.

Who wouldn't want to learn the lesson I learned, he thinks.

What made me the way I am today.

What kind of monster, he thinks.

KNIFE FIGHT

JULIA ELLIOTT

Still bearing scars from multiple stab wounds, Farrell Sprott sat in a nanotech metal chair designed to radiate an uncomfortable chill. The interrogator, Luna Zamora, wore a digital mask that made her resemble an archetypal white aunt, a younger version of Bee from *The Andy Griffith Show*. Detective Noah Banes, a bodybuilder going soft, sat so still that the suspect assumed he was a hologram.

"So you're saying you didn't intend to kill Ken Barnes?" said Detective Zamora.

"That's right, but call him Noid. One: he's paranoid. Two: he's hyper like that old Dominos' cartoon."

"You weren't angry with Noid?"

"Not no more annoyed than usual. He'd brought

over some steaks to sell, and I was trying to fix my Grizzly Hover-Max 660."

"Steaks?"

"Damn expensive GMO mammoth meat. Steals it from the Bi-Lo on Highway 2. Told him I don't eat extinct animals. He said they weren't extinct no more, and then we got to bickering about the meaning of extinction in these times. Next thing you know, we're doing Zoom hits and Beam shots. Lee Jumper, who can smell a party from a mile away, flies up on his Harley Pegasus, which naturally lifts Pauline from her funk. Out she comes, trotting in a pair of hot pants and heels, posting selfies on Piddle while clutching a glass of la-di-da chardonnay. Next thing you know, heathens come zooming out the woods on every make of hover-RV. Noid says, *fuck it, let's grill these mastodon chops.* Erkin Dennis says, *I was gonna sell this dog fentanyl, but you only live once.* Pauline whips off our Jacuzzi cover and pops on her metal classics playlist."

"Dog fentanyl?"

"Meds for canine surgeries. Look, I ain't no narc. Not gonna name no vets. Just trying to show how wasted we were, explain how Noid got stabbed beyond repair."

"What led up to the stabbing?"

"Which one?" The suspect fingers a long keloid on his neck, opens his scar-etched lips, and releases a hiss of dark mirth.

"The one that killed Ken Barnes."

"Carl Mack, who refuses to regenerate and don't trust the OWGCC, started it."

"By which you mean one-world-government-corporate conglomerate?"

"Right. Carl grows half his food, shoots what he can, makes his own shine. Fucker came down from his cabin with an insulated mug of Purple Haze. By then it was 'bout three p.m., hotter than fish grease, making me wonder why the OWGCC can't control the weather. That's why we all had our shirts off, the women in bikinis, three Porta Cools going full blast to fight the swelter. Carl was the first one to whip out his knife, a cold steel Peace Keeper without torpedo tech, 'cause that fucker's au naturel. He hurled it at a squirrel and caught it in the heart. Skinned it right there and slapped it on the grill.

Carl's my man when the apocalypse comes, said Pauline, which, I noticed, put Lee Jumper in a sulk. Next thing I know, Lee's torpedo-hilt Baconmaker's whizzing through the air. Next thing I know, he done caught Noid in the pec by accident, 'cause I swear he was aiming at Carl, who don't have Regeneration™— and everybody knows that would be manslaughter. Noid shrieked, then smiled, then jerked the blade from his body to let the ladies have a look at his blood spurt before the wound closed over. Then Noid shot his Turbo JungleMaster and hit Lee right in the jugular, which made everybody gasp, even though he's got Regeneration Plus. Lee just stood there breathing, eyes filled with weird light. When Pauline rushed to his side, I knew."

"Knew?"

"Knew she was stepping out on me. I imagined them twisted together in the woods at dusk, lightning bugs rising like souls of the unfixable dead. I imagined the way Pauline coos at her happiest time. I hoped Lee's program would malfunction, but Lee Jumper yanked out that toothed dagger. Didn't make a peep as a quart of blood gushed from his neck. Just stood there staring soulfully into Pauline's eyes, his wound pulsing purple and finally white. That's when the dog fentanyl kicked in. I rushed him, and all hell broke loose. It's hard to remember the flow of events."

"Just piece it together the best you can."

"Let's see. I stabbed Lee in the eye, and Lee stabbed me in the neck. On account of adrenaline, opiates, and Regeneration Plus, I didn't feel jack. Didn't feel Erkin's knife hit me in the thigh or Noid's get me in the side. Sensed only a sick grinding pressure as Lee twisted his Baconmaker into my back. I stood up. Saw Noid stab Erkin and Erkin stab Lee. Saw Ronny Timmerman pop from the shadows, shoot his Safari King, and take a slice out of Noid's cheek. Saw Tim Stokes riding R.V. Riddle piggyback while hacking out chunks of flank meat. Saw Irene Timmerman trying to scalp

Crystal Whitaker with a Bear King Blazin' Bowie. Saw Lee stumble to the bushes with so many blades in his back, he looked like a porcupine. And up on the deck was Pauline, going through the seven coordinations of Kyudo, her thigh muscles flexing, an Alpha Wolf Suregrip in each of her capable hands. She leapt from the deck with a tae kwon do kick. As she descended on me in high-res slo-mo, I heard a great racket like the shrieking of many angels. Sadly, Pauline stabbed me in the heart. I felt that white-hot blink of dread that some say is a flash of death before Regeneration pulls you back."

The suspect covered his face with his hands. Detective Banes nodded at Detective Zamora.

The suspect wiped his eyes.

"I stood up bleeding. I stumbled across Bermuda grass dewy with gore and strewn with tidbits of flesh. Among mashed lumps were eyes, ears, fingers, and toes. Friends moaned on the ground, waiting for their wounds to mend. I thought of fallen Confederates in the Battle of Gettysburg, life trickling out of them as clouds of flies descended. I saw Pauline squirming in the muck. Saw Lee and Noid struggling in the hot tub, embraced like lovers, the water churning red. By this point, Noid had no features, just a jellied mask and a howling mouth hole. Pinning his opponent by the neck, Lee sawed at Noid's armpit with a Zero Tolerance serrated blade. Noid didn't squirm, and I

133

knew that Lee intended to take him to the point of no return. So I grabbed a Screaming Eagle that somebody had dropped on the deck. I activated the smart missile feature and flung the weapon toward Lee's broad back. But the bastard was too quick: he pulled Noid on top him, laughed as my weapon pierced the ruined man's heart. Laughed as he murdered Noid in cold blood."

The HVAC system shuddered on. Detective Banes coughed. Detective Zamora refined her digital mask.

"Is that all, Mr. Sprott?"

"I reckon so. Except when Noid went limp I felt a stab of envy, remembering the white-hot light I'd felt, a split second of giddy dread as I shook off my body. But then it came right back."

"What did, Mr. Sprott?"

"That steady weight of sadness."

THE MEME FARM

ADAM McCULLOCH

You like cats? God knows I used to. Make sure to keep your mask on. There's this cat brain parasite, toxoplasma gondii. We're immune of course, but visitors like your good self? Whoa Nelly! So, listen . . . I've got your project in R and D so I'll give you a tour along the way. Mask on? Excellent."

It could be any factory farm but for the fact that it's as clean as a hospital ward. Instead of animal cages, the three-hundred-plus yards of fluorescent tubes illuminate rows of domestic movie-sets: a well-loved lounge, a squalid teenager's bedroom, an overflowing laundry, a man cave, a country kitchen. In each, the fourth wall has been replaced with glass.

"You remember Jeeves the American shorthair?

The cat that swiped that coffee cup off the desk? Jeeves was our first meme. Filmed right here in this lounge-set. It's so realistically crappy, isn't it? Modeled after my apartment, I'm embarrassed to say. Of course Jeeves is long dead now. God, that was insensitive. I'm sorry. You have my deepest sympathies about your boss, you really do. Our best client, bar none. I mean wow . . . what a shock, great dancer . . . that Christmas party."

In the lounge-set strewn with children's toys, a long-haired Persian jams its head in a toy bucket. It forges blindly on, wearing the bucket as a helmet.

"Come to think of it, that's how your department found us. Jeevesy's owner was at the Christmas party down in D.C. Of course there are no 'owners' anymore. We breed everything ourselves. Take this little girl. She's a Cornish rex, specially bred for climbing."

A ribbed red cat climbs the shredded wallpaper, circumnavigating the room using claws as crampons.

"Trust me, you don't want that thing on your lap. Not exactly friendly now that we engineer them. By the way, police took your boss's briefcase, so I hope you weren't expecting any personal effects. They never saw the project he had us working on, of course. I thought it best to return the files to you on the Q.T."

A black-and-white Ragdoll cat is slumped over a Roomba vacuum cleaner as it blindly ricochets around the room. The cat stretches, snagging a low-hanging tablecloth in its claw. It falls on the cat and Roomba, covering both. The Ragdoll doesn't budge.

"Stiff competition nowadays from regular folk with mongrels even, doing all this for free. I guess it achieves the same result but your meme campaign isn't just one cat video. You want thirty memes, minimum, for good media-smothering of anything you don't want reaching the general populace. Hang on, your mask is slipping. Let me fix it."

In a laundry-set, a gray macaque mounts a cheetah and rides it like a jockey.

"Unusual animal pairs are hugely popular. Feds bought a whole bunch for a smothering campaign a while back. The Feds work for you or do you work for them? I can never keep track. Expensive to produce, these memes. We breed the big cats as docile as can be but, deep down, the killer instinct is still there. And everyone wants to go big nowadays . . . cats stealing dog beds just doesn't cut it."

A lab technician hoses out a set resembling a suburban porch. The disemboweled carcass of a Rottweiler oozes blood onto the whitewashed steps. The dog has been eaten down to the spine.

"Sorry. That wasn't meant to be part of the tour. It's part of life, though. One lion means we go through lots of dogs—*loooots* of dogs—until we find one it decides not to eat. Not worth it in my opinion."

In a country kitchen–set, on a floor of black-and-white tiles, baby chickens, each one dyed a pastel hue, all snuggle against the stomach of a black cat.

"This is more like it: great colors, very simple. Who needs lions? We're not trying to win an Oscar. It's about volume. The more memes the better. We did a nice smothering campaign for the NRA. That school shooting, where was it again? Omaha? Ohio? It began with 'O.' Now see that? I can't even remember. That's how successful it was. Wiped the shooting from the news cycle entirely."

Two dozen overweight tabby cats mill around a cartoon bedroom, dragging sagging bellies on the floor.

"How many exotic shorthairs do you think there are here? Twenty? How about one. They're all clones. That's where the real money is. Let me fix your mask. Cat-crazy is one thing, toxoplasmosis is a different story entirely. We filmed twenty identical cats in twenty identical lounge-sets and you know what you've got? A live-action Garfield movie. No visual effects whatsoever."

Tap, tap, tap against the glass. A sudden switch to babyish voice.

"Garfield likes pizza?" In unison the cats line up against the glass and meow loudly, their eyes bulging like Garfield. "Garfield likes Monday?" In unison the cats scowl and slump on the floor. "I just love it when they all 'harumph' together. Wait. Were you at the Christmas party when your boss did the one-arm rumba? That was priceless."

A sign on a locked steel door reads RESEARCH AND DEVELOPMENT.

"Here we are. His death didn't make any sense, though. I mean, the brain stem was missing. Missing!"

The white laminate room is divided in half by a glass wall. On this side a chair and desk, sparsely adorned with a computer and slim folder of paperwork. On the other side, the room beyond the glass appears empty, then the downy head of a naked child appears from behind the desk. The naked child diligently approaches the center of the room, a routine it has followed a thousand times.

"It's not what you think. Let me show you."

The computer comes to life. On screen is the original dancing baby meme from 1996. It wobbles and writhes, arms out, and the naked child follows suit, mirroring every move. The dancing baby wiggles faster and the naked child keeps pace.

"Dancing baby was your boss's idea. You know, to pay homage to the original. It does the mashed potato and pretty good jive. It can't speak or hear, though. Just a giant neural freeway from the eyes to the dancing-shoe part of the brain."

The naked child writhes and grooves.

"You still think it's a child, don't you? I can tell. Well, it's not. It's just like those Garfield cats. If only your boss could have seen it. It's a hu-meme. Get it?"

The naked child dances the mashed potato. And

then it dances the one-arm rumba, just like at the Christmas party.

"Uncanny likeness, isn't it? It's all grown from a donor brain stem. It's not hard to engineer but finding a donor is the difficult part. Your boss was always helpful. Hang on a moment, your mask is slipping. Let me adjust it."

A pair of hands fiddle with the plastic mask. A finger finds a hidden button to press. A sweet smelling toxic gas fills the cup. The room spins and begins to fade. The floor is hard and cool. The naked child dances ever faster.

"This will hurt less if you don't think about it. Just think of cats."

THE RHETORICIAN

ADRIAN VAN YOUNG

hen the man with the accent first called me at home, it stood to reason that he would, for I had placed the number to my cell phone in an ad.

He said: "You're an expert in rhetoric, yes?"

"I teach it," I said, "Once or twice a semester."

The man paused to consider this. "In other words," he said, "an expert."

I met the man outside a dark, cubist building called Inline Education Partners. He was short and rotund with a sweeping mustache. The man drew a textbook from out of his coat titled: *I Say, So What?* "To teach the students in your class."

We crossed through the lobby past a set of elevators whose doors were laced shut with emergency tape.

In the first room were candles that made the walls flicker and men on elevated stools, a few of them drinking espresso from saucers.

"Employee lounge?" I asked the man.

He glanced back at the room. "Ah, that."

In the next room were men standing on tippy toes as they fanned money into a counting machine, and in the third room more men still, working sewing machines over billowing fabric.

In the next and last room was a class full of students. The children were ten to twelve, all boys, with copies of *I Say, So What?* on their desks.

The man with the accent drew near me and whispered: "The sons of the men in our organization. They have district exams coming up. Very nervous. Just between us, you'll say you're a PhD, yes?"

"I'd rather not."

He clapped my back. "Thank you, doctor," he said. "We're extremely obliged."

I led them through argument, premise, conclusion, deductive and inductive logic, comparison. I felt myself bridling to teach from the book, regressive as it sometimes seemed in the rhetoric field, which was always evolving, but the man with the accent had already paid me two months in advance.

When class got out, the man with the accent took my arm. "Good reports coming in from the students," he said. Then he grew faintly awkward. "If you'll come with me."

"May I see the reports from the students?" I said.

"I'd like to take care of some paperwork first."

We entered a room with a gigantic mirror that spanned the back wall end to end.

"If you would," said the man, indicating a chair.

The man left the room and two new men replaced him, escorting a figure contained in a black body bag. The men wore blue suits and white surgical masks.

The body bag's zipper was down a few inches. A third man peered out at me, ashen and mumbling. They sat him across from me, perched on a stool.

"There's a script on the chair," said the man with the accent.

His voice now reached me over speakers, each one to a corner above the glass pane.

I unfolded the several-paged rectangle of it. "Where were you," I said, "on December the ninth?"

"Working for you," said the body-bagged man to the one-sided window along the back wall.

"Address the rhetorician, please."

"Excuse me," I said to the man in the bag. "Where were you the night of December the ninth?"

"At home with my wife and kids," said the man.

I searched the typescript for the answer he'd given: *Subject claims he was home with his family that night.*

I found the correlating question. "Would your family support that?"

"Of course!" said the man. "How can you even ask that? They're my family!"

The script was curious indeed. Beneath all the questions were multiple answers—probable answers to each of the questions decided by the author of the script in advance—and each led the reader to some different question. These questions, in turn, led to more likely answers, like some punitive species of multiple choice.

The script seemed to revolve around someone specific, a man it referred to as Mr. Van Brunt, a person of some upper management, surely, in the organization the man with the accent called Inline Education Partners.

Mr. Van Brunt, who'd been recently murdered.

Mr. Van Brunt, for whom those in the room with the coffee and candles were holding a vigil.

A logic set appeared to me, like a line of dark stones underneath lucid water.

"On the night Mr. Van Brunt was killed," I began, tucking the script beneath my leg, "you say that you were with your family, a fact your family would support, which means you *did not* murder Mr. Van Brunt for no one can be in two places at once?"

"Yes," said the man as he gasped with relief. "That's exactly what I'm saying!"

"Yet being your family," I said, "could they really be said to be telling the truth? In other words, would asking them not be the same as asking you when your family, like you, hold *your* interests at heart?"

The only sound for several moments was the men in the surgical masks breathing roughly.

"Is this man's premise valid," said the man with the accent, "or is his premise questionable?"

"Questionable?" I said.

A pause. The man's voice continued: "Is that your assessment?"

I looked from the glass to the man in the bag. "Questionable, yes," I said.

The masked men converged on the man on the stool: the man on the right zipping up the black bag so his face disappeared and his cries became muffled, while the man on the left held the man in his seat. They drew hammers out of the waists of their pants and beat him about the head and neck in rapid, brutal bursts. He screamed. At the top of the bag where his head would've been, the heads of the hammers began to sound wet.

"May I use the bathroom?" I asked of the mirror.

The bag thrashed a moment. Then slumped to the side.

"Gentlemen," said the man with the accent, "escort him."

I rose and began to advance toward the door, but

the men in the masks turned me back toward the wall. The man on the left raised his hand to the mirror, mumbling under his surgical mask. The wall opened inward, revealing a cot and a small metal toilet that shone with blue slime.

With utter composure, I hunched through the entry and vomited painfully into the hole.

I wiped my mouth and climbed back out, the men in the masks backing out along with me.

The man on the stool had been swapped for another, also in a body bag. His eyes looked at me through a cleft in the zipper.

"Feeling better, I hope?" said the man with the accent.

I nodded grimly at the mirror, but when I turned back to the room, it was gone. The wall was just a wall again.

"That room back there," I said, "whose is it?"

"Why of course," said the man with the accent, "it's yours."

The man on the stool was as pale as the first, but he looked a bit younger. He had darker hair.

"If you would," said the man with the accent.

I sat. A new script was waiting for me on the leather. I folded it out, browsed the question-set there, the variant columns of possible answers.

I said: "Where were you on December the ninth?"

"Excuse me," I said, wiping bile from my mouth.

I never could remember that bit.

"Let me start again," I said. "Where were you *the night* of December the ninth?"

The eyes between the zipper-track turned inward then, desperate and searching. I waited for the mouth to speak the words that could not save its life.

出口なし

中村文則

男が椅子に座っている。

その椅子に、男は覚えがある。男の人生の中で、確かに一度、座ったことのある椅子だった。しかし、どこの店の椅子だったのか、もしくは自分の部屋の椅子だったのか、男は思い出すことができない。

一畳ほどのスペースに、男はいる。男は狭いところが好きではない。そのことも、男は覚えている。目の前にドアがある。そのドアにも覚えがある。でもそれがどこで見たドアなのか、思い出すことができない。

男は椅子に座り、目の前のドアを見続けてい

NO EXIT

FUMINORI NAKAMURA

TRANSLATED BY ALLISON MARKIN POWELL

The man was sitting in a chair.

The chair was familiar to the man. He was certain that this was a chair he had sat in before, at some point in his life. But whether the chair had been in a restaurant somewhere, or in his apartment, the man could not recall.

The room the man was in was about the size of one tatami mat. He did not like confined spaces. The man remembered as much as this. There was a door in front of him. This door was also familiar. But he could not recall where he had seen the door before.

The man sat in the chair, staring at the door in front of him. For what might have been hours, for what

る。数時間かもしれないし、数十年かもしれな
かった。時間の感覚が失われている。ただ、身
体がだるかった。どうしようもないほど、身体が
だるかった。男はうんざりしている。自分の人生
を、常にそう過ごしてきたのと同じように。
　じっとしながら、また数年が経ったような気
がする。この部屋は酷く狭い。音もなく、匂いも
ない。自分が瞬きをしたような気がした時、目の
前のドアがゆっくり開く。男はそのドアの向こう
を気だるく眺める。そこには男が座っている。自
分と全く同じ人間が、こちらをうんざり眺めなが
ら座っている。
　「……そうだと思ったんだよね。……このド
アを開けても、どうせそんなことだろうと」
　目の前の男はそう言う。同じ一畳ほどのスペー
スの中で、開いたドアのすぐ向こうで、男と同
じ姿勢で椅子に座っている。
　「……俺は待ってたんだよ。このドアが開く
のを、ずっと」
　「……俺は迷ってたんだよ。……このドアを
開けるか、ずっと」
　二人の男は、お互いを眺めながら黙る。彼ら
の距離は酷く近い。二人は同じ顔で、同じ服を
着ている。
　「……あのさ、ドアを開けるなら、引いてく
れればよかったんだ。……こちらに押して開け
ただろう？　そうすると、こっちが狭くなる」
　「このドアは押して開けるしかないんでね」

150

may have been years. He had lost sense of time. All he knew was that he felt weary. His body felt impossibly tired. The man was sick of it all. He had spent his entire life feeling this same way.

As he sat there, motionless, it seemed like more years passed. The room was terribly small. There was no noise, no smell. In what seemed like the blink of an eye, the door before him slowly opened. The man gazed languidly at what was on the other side of the door. Another man was sitting there. A person exactly the same as him sat there, jadedly staring back.

". . . Just as I thought . . . If I opened the door, I knew that's what would be there," the man in front of him said. In a room that was the same one-mat size, just on the other side of the door, he was sitting in a chair in the same position as the man.

". . . I've been waiting. For the door to open, all this time."

". . . I've been debating. Whether to open the door, all this time."

The two men stared at each other, without saying another word. The distance between them was terribly close. They both looked the same, they were wearing the same clothes.

". . . Well, so, since you opened the door, I'd appreciate if you would pull it back . . . You pushed it open, right? Now it's even more cramped in here."

"The door only pushes open."

151

　二人はお互いを眺める。

　「……嘘だ。爪先に当たるんだよこのドア
が。引けよ」

　「そういうところだよ。……細かいし、ひと
をすぐ疑う」

　「何言ってるんだよ。……おまえの顔見て
ると苛々するんだよ。……目が暗いんだ。口元
も……、どうにかできないか」

　二人はお互いを盗み見るように、視線を動
かしている。

　「おまえもだよ。……嘘ばかりついてきた。
どれだけの人間を傷つけた？　覚えてるか、あ
の女のことを」

　「……おまえと同じくらいは。他人を幸福に
することからおまえは逃げてきたんだ。挙句の
果てに、無理に会社を起こして、やばい金に手を
出す始末だ。……ん？　おまえ、覚えてるか」

　「……おぼろげに。金を持ち逃げして、マフィ
アに囲まれて……」

　「……ああ」

　目の前の男が息を吐く。

　「……俺達は死んだんだ」

　男が苛立ちながら、こめかみをかく。

　「……なるほど、これが地獄か」

　二人の男は、お互いを眺める。うんざりして
いる。この部屋は酷く狭い。音もなく、匂いもな
い。

　「地獄っていえば、火の海とか、悪魔とか想

152

They both stared at each other.

". . . That's crap. The door's basically touching my toes. Pull it back."

"This is the point . . . You notice everything, you're so quick to suspect."

"What are you talking about? . . . Looking at you pisses me off . . . Your creepy eyes, and your mouth . . . I can't handle it."

Each of them cast furtive glances at the other.

"You should talk . . . All you ever did was lie. How many people did you hurt? Remember what you did to that woman?"

". . . Like you're any better. You ran away from making anyone happy. You're the one who would have done anything to get your business going, even using stolen money in the end . . . Huh? Remember that?"

". . . Vaguely. I remember making off with the money, then being surrounded by gangsters."

". . . Yeah."

The other man exhaled.

". . . We're dead."

The man scratched his temple in irritation.

". . . You're right. This must be hell."

The two men looked at each other. Jaded and exhausted. These rooms were terribly small. There were no sounds, no smells.

"If this were hell, you'd think there'd be a sea of flames, or demons, or whatever . . . You were a loser

像してたけどな……。とにかく、おまえの人生は
失敗だったんだよ。完全な失敗だ。多くの人間を
利用し、傷つけた挙句、成功すらしなかった」
　「そうだ、おまえはやたらと傷つきやすい。
度胸もない。でも野心だけがあった。……自分
の存在の不安を、くだらない野心に変えて」
　二人はお互いを眺める。
　「……なあ、ドアを引いてくれないか。爪先
にドアが当たるんだ」
　「だから、細かいんだよおまえ」
　「引けよ。というか、閉めてくれ」
　「……閉められない。俺も閉めたい。でも、
一度開けたら、もう閉まらないんだ」
　二人の男はしばらく沈黙する。
　「……なら、お互いを見ないようにしない
か？　我慢ならない」
　二人はお互いから目を逸らす。しかし、やはり
目の前の存在が気になって仕方ない。どちらとも
なく、また口を開く。どちらかがこめかみを激し
くかき、どちらかが腰のあたりを酷くかく。
　「……覚えてるか。おまえが裏切った、あの
男を。……え？　どう言い訳する？」
　「おまえが言い訳すればいいだろう。あの
老人のことは覚えてるか？　おまえが金を騙し
取った……」
　二人はお互いを眺める。うんざりしている。
　「……そうか。これが永遠に続くの

154

in life, anyway. A complete and total failure. You used everyone, you ended up hurting all those people, and you weren't even successful."

"Right, but your ego's too damn sensitive. You've got no guts. Nothing but ambition . . . You turned your existential anxiety into worthless ambition."

They both looked at each other.

". . . Hey, would you pull the door? It's touching my toes."

"Like I said, you pay too much attention."

"Pull it! Or just close it."

". . . I can't close it. I wish I could. But now that I've opened it, it can't be closed."

Neither of them said anything for a while.

". . . Then, why don't we try not to look at each other? I can't take it."

Both men averted their eyes. But there was nothing they could do—they knew the other was right there. Each of them opened their mouths again. One scratched his temple roughly, the other rubbed his back intently.

". . . Do you remember? The guy you betrayed . . . Yeah? What'd you do that for?"

"It's okay with you as long as there's an excuse? Remember that old guy? The one you swindled out of his money . . ."

They each looked at the other. They were disgusted.

". . . I see. This goes on forever?"

155

THE HALL AT THE END
OF THE HALL

RYAN BLOOM

The hall in my dream is narrow, the ceiling so high it's out of sight, as if, maybe, it's not even there, the hall not a hall at all but a walled walkway winding toward the sky. My sister, Adèle, loved mazes. Of corn or paper or house or silk, like the one the city erected in Rock Creek Park, near where we lived when we were kids, some sort of art installation, twisting paths lined with orange drapes, as if the dirt trails weren't difficult enough on their own, though the artists had lit the length of the thing, so that from a distance, when the sky went dull and the crickets itched, the scene was like out of some Japanese fairy tale, the drapes like sliding shōji screens, the doors of a hundred tightly packed houses blessing the night, the heat so hot it literally made tar melt.

The house cleaners had a fiesta that summer with all the tar stains they were paid to remove: from the foyers of downtown restaurants and airless Metro cars, from the laundromat on 14th Street where somehow the stains ended up *atop* the machines, and that's not to mention the residential work, the tar-crumb trails from back door to stairs to bedroom. The size-nine shoes. In the entirety of my life, then or since, I've never seen so many women go without bras, the heat too intense even for them. Or that's what I heard Maman tell Papa when he asked why Adèle was "running around *like that*," and why, for that matter, was she, our mother, "running around *like that*, too."

In that summer of tar and heat and mazes, my sister and I must have been, what, sixteen? Seventeen? Young enough, still.

In my dream, the walls of the hall are hung with photographs, Adèle and I on our parents' zebra-striped couch, her sucking *my* thumb; a photo of her at six, beating me in a sack race, head turned as if she were unsure if I were even still with her; at twelve, tongue between teeth, stomach flat against a sheet of paper bigger than her, *literally* bigger, sketching her first "jumbo maze." That's what she called them. "Are you going for Guinness?" I asked the day the photo was taken, but even back then she lived too much in her head to care about such things, what other people thought.

The next photo I pass is much later, post-tarry summer, long after the year we were sixteen and it was hot, hot, hot. A couple of bars out on 18th Street had to close that season because their AC units couldn't keep up and all of their ice had melted and the fridges were no longer cool and who wants to drink warm beer in a warm bar anyway? Apparently there was this one guy with tar-track shoes who kept coming back insisting Guinness was meant to be drunk warm anyway, and so he'd like to stay, but who in their right mind can afford to keep a bar open for one guy and one drink? And anyway, the point is, in the next photograph I pass already my sister's twenty-three, a line of stitches stretching from the pierced nub of her ear up and over her temple, disappearing beneath the blond of her hair, as if something inoperable had been removed—though it hadn't. She's sitting on the zebra-striped couch and I'm sitting next to her, my face turned away. Afraid to look. She'd tried, she said, to get "it" out. "It?" I asked. "It," she said, as if no further clarification were needed, and all I could think of was one of those larval white grubs, but with teeth like in those *Alien* films, the defiled thing writhing around inside her skull, beneath the skin. Chest-busters, they called them in the films, though this one was definitely in her head. A result of what had happened.

159

In the dream, the walls begin to narrow in front of me, and I imagine it might be best to turn back to a time before that summer, the one with the drapery maze in Rock Creek Park. Sycamores and elms. Pawpaws and maples. Cottonwoods. Ironwoods. But mostly ashes. The park was lined mostly with ashes then. White and green. Tall and bulbous and round. A man with size-nine shoes leaning against one, picking at his teeth as if he'd just finished a meal. Adèle's hair, in the photo with the stitches, it's frosted at the tips, the heat having left her long ago, sometime toward the end of that summer before parents worried about bogeymen, when the Park was illuminated in orange silk, a majestic waving wavering at night. Adèle and I often went down in the evening to check out that life-size maze, the heat letting up the tiniest bit then, my sister absolutely set on only one thing: no matter what, we could not break the rules, break through the maze walls, luminous and shimmering, no matter how lost we got, we would not be like *those* kids. *We* would follow the paths. Make Ariadne proud. Even if a Minotaur should appear, stamping his hoofs of tar, picking meat from his teeth, still we would not cheat.

Our family had to hire the house cleaners, too, that summer, to erase sixteen size-nine footprints from the hall where Adèle's enormous roll of maze paper had spread, eight tar-prints tracking from the steps to her room, eight tracking back down. We weren't crazy about locking our doors that year, but who was then—it was so, so hot, and though I've never believed Washington qualifies as the South, it does get scorching like down there, and we had a magnolia tree in our front yard like they do, perfumed white petals dropping all over the place, and the screen doors to the house were made of slatted wood and had transoms overtop to keep the air moving, and so, yes, okay, I get it: call an elephant an elephant. Especially if it's in the room. We'd seen the guy before, Adèle said, later. He'd followed her around the day we split up in the Rock Creek maze, he sipping a can of warm Guinness. It was because our mother had let her, "a young woman in full bloom," run around without a bra, our father said. "Didn't I tell you," he said. "It's because I let us get separated," I said.

And said.

And said.

"What an awful mess," one of the cleaners said. "I have a daughter, too."

In my dream, when I reach the door, the walls are so constricted I can barely move, barely budge my arm, barely get my hand up to open it, but I do, finally, clench my fingers around the knob, praying for escape, for space to breathe. For my sister. The doorjamb encrusted with grubs and browned magnolia leaves. But when I push the portal open, on the other side, there's only another door and another hall, and another hall and another hall at the end of the hall, at the end of the hall another hall, hall hall all the way through.

161

FRIENDS

LAURA VAN DEN BERG

Sarah had moved to a city of medium size, the worst size for making friends. A place is a place, she told herself, but she had never before lived in a city of medium size. People were moderately friendly. The streets moderately busy. Everything moderately expensive and moderately good-looking. She lived near a park with cannons and an American flag, the most patriotic park she'd ever seen. Beyond the park lay a river of moderate width, slicing through the city like a silver vein.

She was not a friendless person. In fact, she had plenty of friends, from cities big and small, and some of these friends offered to set her up with people they knew in the medium city. The site of her first friend date was a restaurant trying very hard to look like it belonged to a larger city. Sarah spotted the friend's friend sitting at the bar, drinking a luminous green cocktail. She was sporty-beautiful, the kind of woman who could be glamorous in sweats because everything was of such fine quality. Sarah disliked her on sight and left immediately. On the street she sent a text. *Sorry! Food poisoning!* The friend texted back right away, with sympathy, and Sarah never replied.

On the second attempted friend date, Sarah, after two beers, started talking about her mother. Her mother had visited recently and insisted on staying in a hotel. It did not matter that Sarah, for the first time in her life, had rented an apartment with a guest room. It did not matter that she had promised to clean the bathroom. Her mother said she did not feel safe staying with Sarah. Her own mother! At the bar, this one communist-themed, the second friend shredded a cocktail napkin, a mural of Lenin peering over her shoulder. Sarah went to the bathroom and by the time she returned, the friend had paid her share and left.

The third friend suggested meeting in a park. Odd, since they were getting together after work, but then again she hadn't had much luck in indoor spaces. Aided by the flashlight app on her phone, Sarah found this woman, Holly, sitting on a bench in an eggplant-colored trench coat.

"You found me," Holly said. "That's a good sign."

A sign of what exactly Sarah did not think to ask.

Before long she was recounting the story about her mother's visit. She knew this was off-putting but could not help herself—did not want to help herself, perhaps. Holly didn't leave or change the subject. Instead she said, "I can see your mother's side of things."

"You've never met my mother," Sarah said. "You don't know anything about us."

"All I need to know is what's right in front of me," Holly said, with a shrug.

Sarah wanted to argue, but when she went to compile evidence to demonstrate that she was indeed a person others could feel safe with, she came up very short.

She and Holly continued seeing each other, always outside and at night. They played tennis at the courts by the library. They went for runs along the river. By April, Sarah had lost five pounds. "You're the perfect friend," Holly said once, in the moonlight. The statement struck Sarah as half-finished, like there was another piece Holly was holding back, but she wasn't used to compliments and it felt ungracious to push for more.

One Saturday morning, Holly sent a text asking if Sarah wanted to meet at the train station. *Up for an adventure?* Sarah was pleased; spending time in the daylight seemed like a friend-promotion. On Platform 6, she found Holly leaning against a concrete pillar in her eggplant trench, holding a round leather case by its handle.

165

"I got us two tickets." She passed one to Sarah. The destination had been crossed out with black marker. Holly gave Sarah the window seat, and as the train chugged away from the medium-size city she pressed her palms to the glass and thought of the succulents lined up in her windowsill—waiting, she imagined, for her to come home.

They rolled past Trenton, Philadelphia, Baltimore. Big cities. They drank coffee and ate BabyBels. When Sarah asked after their destination, Holly just said, "We have a ways to go." By the time they hit Washington the sun was melting across the sky. In Alexandria, Holly made another trip to the café car, and returned carrying a cardboard tray packed with little red wines and hummus cups. She handed the tray to Sarah and collected her round case. She said it was time to go to the roomette.

"This is an overnight?" Sarah said, frowning.

"We have a ways to go," Holly said again.

The roomette held bunk beds and the smallest toilet Sarah had ever seen. She sat on the bottom bunk. Holly joined her, the round case wedged between her feet, and unscrewed a little wine.

"That city was not a good size," Holly said. "The people who built it should have stopped sooner or made more."

Sarah was troubled by the past tense, as though the city had ceased to exist upon their departure.

"You won't miss it much," Holly added, handing her the bottle.

Sarah closed her eyes for a moment, felt the sway of the train.

"Are you *kidnapping* me?"

"Do you see a gun? Can a friend kidnap a friend?" Holly laughed and punched her in the shoulder. Sarah killed the bottle, one eye trained on the round case. She imagined a weapon rattling around inside.

"Seriously, though, I can't start over in a new place without a friend," Holly said. "Can you imagine?"

"Yes," Sarah said. "I can."

"You, my dear, are a cautionary tale." Holly loosened the belt on her trench.

"I should call my mother." By then the land around the tracks had gone dark.

"Forget about your mother," Holly said. "She doesn't want to hear from you."

In Hamlet, North Carolina, they climbed into the bunk beds. Sarah took the top, the ceiling so close she felt as though she'd been sealed inside a carapace. A little while later Holly's voice floated up from the floor.

"So what happened with your mother? I'd like to hear about it in your own words."

Last year, Sarah had moved in with her mother to help her recover from a double knee replacement, an arrangement that brought out the worst in them. Her mother had a little silver bell she rang every two minutes. Every way Sarah tried to help was wrong.

167

She got the wrong things at the grocery. She always forgot to refill the bedside water glass. One afternoon she locked her mother's door from the outside. She listened to the chiming bell. After thirty minutes, she unlocked the door. She claimed to have been out of earshot in the backyard, but they both knew. The next day she left a sandwich and a half-glass of water at her mother's bedside, locked up, and went to see a movie.

"Let's just say things did not improve from there." Sarah thought it was close to midnight, though she couldn't be sure because her watch had stopped in Cary. Her phone had died too, and none of the chargers in the roomette were working.

"Am I a terrible person?" Sarah asked.

"Yes," Holly said. "That's what makes you perfect."

Sarah asked Holly if she had brought a friend with her to the medium-sized city—and, if so, what had become of this person. In response, Holly began to snore loudly.

Sarah supposed she would get her answer soon enough.

Next door a toilet flushed. Someone was having a sneezing fit. When she tried to remember the friend who set her up with Holly, she failed to summon a name. But surely this person existed—otherwise how would they have found each other? She imagined this friend in the roomette next door, whispering through an air vent.

The next stop was called Denmark, South Carolina.

Sarah rolled toward the wall. She listened for the voice of her friend, who she hoped would explain that while Holly had strange ideas about what constituted adventure she was really quite harmless, but that was not the voice she heard. Instead it was her mother, saying something about a bell.

MINOR WITCHCRAFT

CHIARA BARZINI

ulieta la Bruja and I arrived at the wedding party inside the modern art museum. We had decided early on that our mission was to spoil the celebration for the bitch bride and her blond friends. They had haunted our adolescence and we were back for revenge. We arrived drunk, already causing a stir. We just didn't give a fuck. We headed straight for the most prestigious room. Julieta la Bruja recognized our childhood friend, walked over to her, and told her what she thought: that she belonged on the streets of Tijuana.

I sat in the middle of the room like a real witch,

focusing on what spell might cause the biggest uproar: How did one go about really ruining someone's wedding? Julieta la Bruja held court with a smirk on her face walking the frightened guests down a dangerous memory lane: "Remember when you teased me and said I was an orphan? Remember when you invited me to a birthday party that didn't exist? Remember when you force-fed me *dulce de leche* saying I was fat?"

The well-groomed girls in the corner of the room, De Chiricos hanging above their heads, shook their heads no. They had blocked all of it out.

I figured that when hatred really flowed, people usually burned things down. I filled a tank with gasoline and dipped my long, golden fingernails inside. Each time I extracted them, I shook the oily liquid into the corners of the room on an incendiary kick. I didn't want to pour it. We wanted everything to happen little by little, like real torture. Julieta la Bruja lit a match and threw it on the ground dramatically. Okay, fine, it wasn't exactly like in the movies, where the whole perimeter of the room caught fire in a second, but things got interesting when we began to spray the gasoline directly onto the squirming guests.

"Set them on fire!" Julieta la Bruja commanded.

We managed to cause a half-assed human combustion and ran away. The wedding people came after us. Outside, in a gas station by the parking lot, stood a huge, tubular truck. We set that on fire also.

"To make things more epic," Julieta la Bruja explained.

The flames spread. The guests chased after us with chopsticks from their Malaysian hors d'oeuvres and fire extinguishers at hand. Julieta la Bruja and I took shelter behind the blazing gas station. From a broken window we looked at the screaming blondes running past us, bile foaming at their mouths, and soon enough we too would combust.

THREE SCORES

NICK MAMATAS

He knows you're not going to call the police," Barb said.

"He's right about that." D'shawn was sitting in the reclining chair in the middle of the darkened living room. He liked to think of it as his captain's chair. He liked to imagine the small house was the starship *Enterprise*, and the bay window through which Barb, on her knees, was looking at the viewscreen. She was even reporting what she saw, just like on the show, despite the fact that D'shawn had a clear view of Finn, Barb's ex, on the lawn. Finn had just undone his belt and thrown his wallet to the ground. It bounced, flew open, and spread a variety of cards and slips of paper everywhere.

"Come on out and face me!" Finn said. His shirt came off. Dad bod. Not that D'shawn's body was much better, but he was bigger. "Don't make me use the N-word!"

Barbara cringed, but D'shawn burst out laughing.

"Look, he's going to ruin business unless you get rid of him," Barb said, suddenly all business herself. D'shawn had two businesses, and one of them was dealing drugs out of his house. Barb was there for some. The other, less savory, involved comic books, action figures, and a mix of replica and occasionally actual championship belts from defunct professional wrestling promotions. That's how D'shawn had first met Finn.

"All right," said D'shawn, pulling his pants up.

Finn was stalking back and forth across the little bit of lawn in front of D'shawn's house like an impatient cartoon character. D'shawn threw his arms up and said, "'Tsup!"

"You . . ." Finn pointed. "I figured it out. I'm no fucking cuck, not anymore."

"Is this some right-wing bukkshit you got from the Internet?"

"The problem is that you have nothing to lose, D'shawn," Finn said. "Or think you don't."

"That's the exact opposite—"

"Shut the fuck up." Somehow Finn had a thick yuppie kitchen knife in hand now. D'shawn felt something surge in his body, like his central nervous system was trying to run back into the house without his flesh, his bones—like he had already been filleted.

"I's the kind of guy who maxes out my 401k contributions, D'shawn. I have a portfolio. I'm a winner." He patted his stomach. "Your retirement plan is a set of first-run, mint, unopened, WWF Wrestling Superstars bendable action figures." Finn was a fan of old-school rasslin; he'd always hated Hulk Hogan and eighties grappling.

"What's your point, dude?" D'shawn asked, half to keep Finn talking, half to remind himself that the point was at the end of Finn's knife. Fucking Barb, telling him to go outside and deal with this shit. They should have both just quietly left out the back door, or waited for Finn to get bored and go home.

"My point is that I was fucking afraid of you, but I'm not afraid anymore. I had too much to lose. What if you punched me in the face and I had to get dental implants?" Finn said. "My credit rating was too high, until now, to deal with you and get Barb back."

"Oh Christ, did you read *Fight Club* finally?" D'shawn decided that he was ready to get stabbed; this was all just too fucking absurd.

"I maxed out my credit, all my cards, for fun. I stopped paying the mortgage. Fuck the bank. It'll take them months to foreclose. Let them drag me out of there."

"You think Barb is going to want to be homeless

with you?" D'shawn asked. "Even if this . . . uh, spectacle works out how you want?"

Finn took a step closer. D'shawn knew he should back up one, keep the distance at least three paces apart, but he couldn't bring himself to. Front-yard shouting contests were hardly rare in his neighborhood, but only a bitch would let the interloper win. D'shawn liked his fights highly choreographed and live on Monday nights, or at least sans blades. He was running out of options.

"Barb, get out here!" he called out, over his shoulder. "You better come the fuck out here!" he shouted when he didn't hear his screen door creak open.

"Do you know your credit score, Dee-shawn?" Finn asked. "Did you even know that there are three major credit agencies? The difference between FICO and VantageScore? My scores were licking 800. Three credit scores, and you can bet that any lender will take the one that's 690 more seriously than the two that are 745. I have a fucking app that wakes me up at five a.m. whenever my score changes. It's been beeping a lot lately. I've been ruining myself so I can do this. Nothing left to lose."

"Finley, get the hell out of here!" Barb shouted. "I told you, I want you out of my life. D'shawn is gonna kill . . ." She stopped in her tracks when she saw the knife. She had a baseball bat in her hands. It had been signed by somebody. D'shawn had two reasons to suck his teeth.

And a third. Now doors and windows were opening. Two kids on their razor scooters had just stopped on the corner to watch and giggle. White people with weapons was something to see on a Sunday morning. At least all the proper old ladies were at church.

"Let's go inside and talk this over," said D'shawn. "You can stab my ass inside, Finn. You'd like that, right? You and Barb could have make-up sex on the couch. Just roll me off of it and grab a towel." D'shawn's tongue surprised his brain.

"Put the bat down, cunt," Finn said. There was flint in his voice now. A car rolled over the lip of the driveway, then stopped, slowly reversed, and drove off with the three hundred dollars D'shawn was going to make today. Finn turned to watch.

D'shawn thought about charging. A spear, like Edge's, Rhyno's, Goldberg's. He'd seen them do it a million times. He glared at Barb, willing her to *fucking do something*. Let her take the cut. Celibacy could be cool. Shaolin monks were celibate.

"The bat," Finn said. "Put it the fuck down."

"I've got range on my side," Barb said. She pointed the bat at him like a sword.

"That's not . . . don't . . ." D'shawn said to Barb. He should just push her at her husband and run, he thought.

"Range." Finn snorted. "I'm the one in range." He turned the knife on himself, gripped the blade with both hands, and pushed.

"Fuck!" D'shawn lunged to grab the knife, then heard a howl and felt the bat crack across his back.

"Let him do it!" Barb shouted. She raised the bat overhead like an axe. D'shawn had the knife. There was blood, but not a lot. He caught a flash of something out of the corner of his eye and recognized it—the metal scallops of Lou Thesz's skinny, circa-1957 NWA–heavyweight championship belt around Finn's waist. The knife had knicked Finn, but not sunk deep. Finn was on his knees, arms snaking around D'shawn's neck.

D'shawn could stab him, get brained by Barb. Stab Barb, get choked by Finn. Kobayashi Maru, he thought. What would Kirk do?

THE ODDS

AMELIA GRAY

He had seen her around for months, but first gathered up the courage to speak to her the day he found her sunbathing on the roof of the apartment complex.

"You'll catch cancer doing that," he said.

"I hope I do," she said.

He immediately asked her out.

At dinner, she ordered the meat loaf smothered in gravy with a side of sliced bologna and turtle cheesecake and ate it all grimly.

"Do you really think it will work?" he asked. She looked very slim, as if the processed meat slid right through her.

"It might be collecting in my heart," she said. "I could look perfectly happy until it happened."

"That's how it was with my aunt. But wouldn't you rather not be part of some sad statistic?"

She sliced a thick triangle of bologna. "You're a statistic either way," she said. "You were saying, you took up diving?"

He'd hired a boatman who didn't remark on all the bloody meat he brought with him in a cooler, and only frowned and looked away when he dumped the contents of the cooler into the water and went in after. "I thought for sure it would work," he said. "But I didn't get so much as a nibble from a grouper, let alone a shark."

"Maybe it was the wet suit. You could try it somewhere warmer, where you can have more flesh exposed. Some place tropical, lots of falling coconuts."

He considered this. It would cost him another month's salary, but what was the point of making money if not to spend it? He wasn't the type who hoarded funds to eventually give to his children, who didn't exist at the moment, and if they ever did, would probably live in a society where currency had no meaning. The odds were good.

"I would love to see you again," he told her at the end of the night.

"Seems likely," she said, lighting her next cigarette with the last. She offered him another drag, but he passed it up. Too easy.

○

They were newlyweds when the carnival came to town. They walked to the fairgrounds holding hands. She sipped alternately between a soda and a beer as he considered the different rides. A kiddie roller coaster worked its way around a track in low dips. Children ran in and out of a fun house, with two-way mirrors and slanted floors. Towering above it all, a creaking metal contraption threw its passengers from one side of a metal bench to the other while they shrieked, holding a single padded bar for safety.

"That one," he said.

She frowned up at it. "I'll stay here."

"Come on, it will be fun. And you never know."

She held his soda while he waited his turn for the metal tower. A family of four was ahead of him, and when it came time to board, the five of them were seated together on the bench.

"When I was a little girl, one of these flew off its rails at the highest point," the mother said. "It went thirty feet before landing on top of a batting cage." Her children were shoving each other and screaming. "I told them the story, but kids don't care. They kept saying they wanted to ride the thing that looked like a fidget spinner, and finally I was like, whatever."

"Tell me more about the accident," the man said. "Did anyone die?"

The ride groaned, shuddering as it lifted from the ground. "I'm going to be sick," the mother said.

The man felt his heart beating. He slid to the edge

of the bench, felt the edge of his body press into the open gap between the seat and the bar. But he couldn't make himself do it on purpose. Far too common. And so the ride progressed without incident, and other than the pleasure of the mother screaming for her life beside him, there was no fun in it.

His wife was sitting on the bench where he left her. It was a filthy bench, a kind of corroded old iron which had been painted a thousand times and covered with all manner of carnival detritus. She was running her hands across the metal and licking her fingers.

"How was it?"

"Fine." He was in a sour mood. "Let's go."

They watched the children running around: children with runny noses, with cotton candy and balloons, with strange raised rashes. "I wonder if any of these kids have measles."

"Is measles still even a thing?" he asked.

"More often than you'd think."

She waited until they were standing on their porch to get into it. "It would have happened years ago if you weren't so precious about it," she said.

He gritted his teeth, but couldn't ignore the bait. "Is this about my diet?"

"It's much easier for men who eat meat," she said.

○

"Hard liquor. Processed cheese. You have such an ego."

"At least I am trying to ascribe some meaning to it."

She scoffed. "You just want to be on the news."

After she went in, he stood under the dead oak tree for another hour, waiting for a heavy branch to fall on him.

They preferred to make their own improvements on the house rather than calling a contractor, though she liked the idea of strangers having an extra key. He insisted on doing all the painting. She tried halfheartedly to trip over a few loose plywood boards and at one point sampled a bit of the paint, but gave up and returned to the couch.

"You all right?" he asked, holding the ladder with one hand as he leaned over the stairwell to get a spot almost out of reach.

"It's difficult," she said. "I always thought once I started really trying, it would be easy."

He came down off the ladder. "It was never going to be easy," he said.

She wouldn't look at him. On TV there was a report of a fire, twenty miles away but growing. Two hundred homes were in danger. The report showed firefighters working their way across smoldering brush. He felt her tense up.

"I need to go," she said. She went into the bedroom and came out in a beautiful red dress, a thin one that caught the sunlight and turned her shadow golden.

185

"Wait," he said. "Don't do this. It should be special for you."

"Everything is *special*," she said, the word ugly in her mouth. And she was gone.

He didn't hear from her after that, and though there was no report, he knew it had worked. He thought that would be the end of it and mourned in a quiet way, using a broomstick to drape her clothes into the lower branches of the old dead oak tree.

But that wasn't the end of it, not quite. A few weeks after the fire was contained, the city investigators found a woman's body near the worst of it, a perimeter of gasoline proof enough that she had played some part. They showed an aerial view on the news, and though her remains had been removed, it was possible to see their outline in the clearing, arms spread in the center of a charred halo of accelerant.

The reporter describing the scene fell silent, and when her voice returned it was choked with emotion. "It's almost beautiful," she said, stammering off script. "The way she's so perfectly presented. It's so unusual. Stunning, really. Investigators will be studying this for years to come."

The man reached forward to touch the screen. The ashes of flesh and wood, the outline of her body seared into the earth. It was the most beautiful death he had ever seen. She would have hated it, hated it!

NOBODY'S GONNA
SLEEP HERE, HONEY

DANIELLE EVANS

Veronica admits there was a moment when she thought this was going to be glamorous. Everything was only just beginning to go to hell: walls and checkpoints going up, a scattershot of environmental disasters, self-declared militias on patrol. It seemed like a good plan they had, to be on a boat for a while. It was the kind of idea people had early on, when it still seemed possible that it would end soon enough and well enough, when the present seemed like an opportunity to make history. The kind of story a plucky filmmaker would love twenty years from now: mild-mannered booksellers become pirate librarians! A thing they could tell their grandkids.

The pirate business was mostly theoretical. Performance art as much as anything. They raised the money for the boat on GoFundMe and bought it cheap from a photographer with dual citizenship who had decided to wait things out in Europe. It was a boat and not a ship, even after they painted it and gave it a handmade flag. They were going to sail the great loop, hang out doing banned-book readings from port to port, then go home and fund-raise for part two, a more elaborate trip involving cutting through Panama and sailing up the west coast. At one of the early read-ins they wore pirate costumes, but only because the local community theater had donated them at their launch party.

They wanted to promote reading and storytelling and art and truth and for three months that was considered safely theatrical because mostly it was, and in the fourth month a border patrol boat shot at them when they tried to pull in to the national harbor. So, no more storytimes. Now they actually traffic in illicit text. Medical texts to the hospital and women's health books, banned books to people who promise to safely spirit them to other countries, notes and encryptions from one underground group to another. Veronica has learned to shoot, though she has not yet shot at anything discernible. Guns are easier to get now than ibuprofen. Grace has learned to home-brew beer on deck, which is worth more than money in certain circles. By the end of the first year they were on the terrorist watch list, which means there are no more safe ports, not officially. Their passports got them in anywhere once, but now most countries assume that a U.S. citizen at their borders is on the run from something.

Veronica has been on the boat or hiding out on isolated beaches long enough that the sun has darkened her skin to a color she'd never known it was capable of in the Midwest. In the first years the coasts had been riskiest, but now that it was not so much a country people tried to get into, inland was the bigger problem. There are zones she can't legally go into anymore as a black woman, and even in the safe zones she could be asked any time for a passport or travel pass. When they must go into the interior for something, Grace does it and Veronica waits. She misses highways. She misses rest stops and artificial color and tasteless deep fried food and her body before it went skinny and feral, misses especially her formerly magnificent breasts.

She misses her daughter.

Lyla couldn't be on a boat during the school year, Adam said, and it was only going to be for a little while, Veronica said. Which was a way of leaving, which was a way of not talking about the state of the country or their marriage. They'd spent the year before the election screwing away their anxiety. The barista and Lyla's swim coach and the woman who'd been in charge of the losing campaign's local office (him). The visiting journalist and the bartender and the philosophy professor (her). Hard to say who'd been wronged first but clear they each believed it to be themselves. He thought she was being paranoid about what would happen next. She thought he was spoiled and stupid for not taking her seriously. He could have slept with an entire coffee shop's worth of baristas if he'd plan for the worst with her, was her view, though he did not seem to reciprocate it. The year they met she got a tattoo of a poem he recited to her on their second date. Their second date was in the cafeteria of a hospital where each of them had a parent dying. It was also the location of their first date and the place where they met. A tattoo is not a scar, it is a wound that never heals. A mild state of permanent infection.

They saw each other a few times. In Florida she had put on a cap and a fanny pack and gone to Disneyworld to meet them. Lyla lit up seeing her, lit up the park with her excitement about being in a place where you could still call the fear and shifting ground magic. Lyla was sunlight and laughter and Veronica's beating heart, but also her face, her spitting image except Adam-colored, except pale and blond and happy. Still, it felt wrong. She and Adam whispered in the fear of their hotel room that the trip had been a bad idea. The next time they were on their way back up north and Veronica could still cross borders, so they met in Canada. He looked at her like he did when they met; looked at her like she was oxygen and clean water.

The tech companies took sides and wireless signals

were spotty for months. When she finally got through they were off the keys somewhere and Adam was all bad news. The city was out of clean water again and bottled was limited. There was some kind of new drug and it was bad. The teachers had been fired from Lyla's school, which would reopen next week with new, properly vetted teachers.

"We're going home," he said.

That he was cryptic meant he must have thought someone else was listening, but he also knew what she would hear. Adam's mother is dead, his father remarried and living in a safe zone, a zone that voted for all of this, a zone that even on a pass Veronica can't enter now.

"You can't take Lyla there," she said. It was a statement of fact or it was a plea.

"I can," he said.

He could. She knew that. She knows that. Her daughter is white until more months of summer sun than she will see on land, until someone sees her with her mother, until someone asks the right question and she forgets to lie. Even in what used to be her normal life, something in Veronica had suspected it would come to this, that even in the country she grew up in, no one who didn't have to would in their right mind choose to claim her forever. Every time Grace comes back from the inside it is a small miracle. Veronica is on a boat. Somewhere in what used to be her country, her daughter is a white girl. Somewhere in who used to be her daughter, she is a ticking bomb.

THE WRONG ONE

ERICA WRIGHT

Leeches should have been the least of my concerns, but I put on my waders anyway. *Ophelia*, I thought, looking at the girl's hair rippling away from the back of her head. But the water was too shallow, and I knew that her face would be scraped and bruised from the rocks.

"Ain't rattlers, Dee, just horned-up crickets."

The newest member of the volunteer fire department had a too-big wad of chaw in his cheek and was spitting often enough to make a circle in the weeds at his feet. He didn't seem to care that he was the bull's-eye. Ardy's bravado didn't surprise me, but hanging around in the sticks past eighteen? There must have been some girlfriend, but I couldn't think who was near enough his age to matter.

The water bubbled past the rubber of my boots and kept going toward Nashville, sixty miles or forever, depending on who you asked. She was heavier than I would have guessed, and my hands slipped on the first try. The water splashed onto my pants, and I tried not to think *death water*. I bent from my knees and locked my arms around her torso, hauling us both upright with a grunt. Dee started vomiting behind me, but I didn't turn around, walking backward one step at a time. The corpse's hair was in my mouth, and I made myself think *girl's hair* instead. Neither Dee nor Ardy helped me when I got to the bank, and I had to drag her by the arms onto the mud and shells. Crawfish darted back into the water.

"Well," Ardy asked.

"It's not her," I said.

He spat toward the ground, but a black glob got stuck to his cheek, and he wiped it off. Dee came crashing into view, shrieking about snakes again. Sure enough, when I turned to where she was pointing, a cottonmouth was burning through the water.

"She got ID or something," Ardy said.

"Dog tags around her neck," I said.

"No shit!"

I shook my head, more irritated with myself for making a joke than with Ardy. "She's got nothing on her."

Nobody said anything for a while, then Dee suggested we pray or something. She just wanted to go home, though. I stripped off my dishwashing gloves and shoved them into my pocket, nodding. Something would eat her if we didn't tell anyone she was here.

I kept my boots on as we headed back the way we came, through an overgrown field belonging to a neighbor long past retirement age. Dee walked close enough behind me to catch my heels from time to time. She smelled sick, and I figured she'd tell her husband she'd been drinking. Ardy's parents wouldn't care that he'd been gone all afternoon, and there was nobody waiting for me. Maybe next time, it would be the right girl.

THE TRASHMAN COMETH

J. W. McCORMACK

The Trashman travels in the back of his truck, rather than the front like other gatherers of refuge, and seldom does anyone see the shrouded figure behind the wheel when he pulls up the curb and opens the compactor. The Trashman slips out with his bag. His face is a frozen mask that neither smiles nor frowns. But his bag smiles, crinkly plastic hungry for its diet of secret things. Life must have room for improvement. The present must have space. The Trashman starts with the mailbox, padding the bottom of his bag with court summonses and magazine subscriptions. Things no one cares about, as opposed to the things everyone has forgotten. For those, he must crawl in under the windowsill and sneak into the bedroom, where he wriggles

under a spare mattress, where he tiptoes around the
conjugal bed and fishes between the cushions. His bag
waits outside, yawning for the waste and trinkets the
Trashman tosses out the window. He pilfers painful
memories and good ones that have no open circuit in
the present. His service is useful, but his aspect is terrible; if you were to wake while he slid pictures from
their frames you would imagine yourself inside the grip
of a weird nightmare. Children sleep as the Trashman
crouches on their bed frame and siphons the physical
residue of their youth. Without the Trashman, no one
can grow any older. He snatches up macramé made at
summer camps and photographs of beachside vaca-
tions, ferrets out hidden postcards, and as he fills his
bag, the memories associated with each object erode.
The sleeper awakens into a life made a little smaller,
a little more manageable, sheared of a little unneces-
sary pain and needless sentiment. The Trashman's bag
bulges with secrets.

Like all angels of mercy, the Trashman's duties
are prescribed by a higher power. But the manner in
which he carries them out are open to his discretion.
He sometimes pauses to admire a compromising photograph or a pressed flower. Should he rid this woman of
the stuffed rhinoceros she bought for a child that went
unborn? Or unspool the tape from this mixtape, traded
for a sagging ex-rebel's ancient virginity? He parts his
pale lips and out comes his long tongue, tasting each

object in turn and weighing its value. If it is sour, it is truly forgotten. It is less than trash and of no interest to this Trashman. But if it is sweet, then it still has the power to stir. The power to disturb the present with the reverberations of the past. Then it goes into the bag.

And then there are the houses of the dead, or houses that are themselves dead and gone. He squelches all needless things that stain the earth and, without the Trashman, would overcrowd it. These dead souls he takes wholesale, unbuilding what the living have accrued. Every piece of furniture, every unrealized dream. The bag has room enough for everyone.

And so the Trashman journeys from house to house, lugging his huge bag behind him. The truck follows at a distance. Time moves differently for the Trashman and the days are like cracked plates that he splits straight through. He'll cover the whole Earth in a week, following the night. The night is his harvest season. Sometimes he carries a scythe, for when he must cut a precious piece of detritus from hands that clutch at it, instinctively protecting the objects that make their lives impossible. But the bag will be fed and so the Trashman gorges it on abacuses, rocking horses, mailboxes, lipstick, lip gloss, pinups, teacups, footstools, bridges, ladders, letter openers, spoons, globes, bicycles, unicycles, ice-cube trays, bales of hay, stereos, sextants, plungers, dials, eyeglasses, astrolabes, LPs, toothpaste, mill wheels, marbles, milk cartons, fire alarms, andirons, sofas, portraits, cradles, coffins, keyboards, surfboards, handlebars, bells, desk chairs, chaise lounges, bookcases, diamonds, pearls, inhalers, pillboxes, top hats, tiles, chimneys, washing machines, telegraphs, candlesticks, bowling balls, walking sticks, sunglasses, shot glasses, rifles, printers, neckties, Coke bottles, beer cans, air conditioners, jukeboxes, music boxes, cereal boxes, heart-shaped boxes, balloons, chains, cages, collars, wigs, hand mirrors, light switches, Christmas trees, go-carts, engine parts, stethoscopes, wooden crates, trash cans, necklaces, funnels, cranes, model planes, shovels, pencils, rubber stamps, books on tape, quills, shower stalls, Matryoshka dolls. In a list that goes on forever, he drains the world of its sinks, shells, feathers, faucets, baskets, bones, bathtubs, TV sets, marionettes, petals, paper dolls, china dolls, honeycombs, wheels, windups, matchbooks, storybooks, lampshades, stuffed birds, keys, wrappers, blankets, crosses, fences, fortunes, doorknobs, doghouses, street signs, cuckoo clocks, board games, bedposts, stepping stones, camera cases, film reels, lawn gnomes . . . and never, in all this flotsam, has he found what he is looking for.

ACTUAL URCHIN

HENRY HOKE

The way the urchin died was he walked up to a guy and said you owe me fifty bucks and the guy stabbed him in the heart.

The way the urchin died was he went into a bar fuming and grabbed a guy that owed him money and said where's my money and the guy killed him right then and there.

The way the urchin died was he lent the wrong guy money, and that guy turned out to be a killer. His killer.

This was way after the old days, way after he was famous. Way after.

The studio needed an actual urchin. They were tired to death of show kids. This new production was scrappy. It needed that shit-on mood, spines at its center.

Men from the gate went out to drag the streets like dog-catchers and come back with candidates. Not too sick, said the studio. We can't work with sick.

There was only one true choice. They found the actual urchin standing on a dead-end street, looking up at a lamppost like it was the sun.

Action, the director would shout from his chair, and the urchin would take charge, bringing the show kids down to his level for mischief and puppy love. The studio had a hit show on their hands. They kept the urchin in-house.

At the end of the shoot day, which was every day except Sunday, drunk parents would come and scoop up their show kids and the urchin would head back to his room in the basement. There'd be soup waiting and no windows and he'd dream of a dugout. Of a cool lagoon.

202

The urchin never knew what to say, unless someone told him.

Not for a billion bucks, he would say.

You're trouble, he would say.

Boy would I, he would say.

We've all seen him. We all know.

A ton of time can pass during a commercial break.

Motherfuck, said the director one day through his old-timey megaphone. They said motherfuck, even back then. You're too big a boy now, you can go. Plus you're starting to break out in hives, maybe it's the oil we use to slick your hair, maybe it's—

They sent him out the back gate. He got an apartment one block away and started drinking and borrowing money and doing all the other fun things big kids do. There was a clause in the urchin's contract that once released he couldn't lead a happy life.

How's he doing? those that thought of the urchin or saw him in reruns would ask. Is he even alive? I think so, whoever would reply. And for a decade and a half, whoever was right. Until one day they weren't.

203

How did the urchin die, they'd ask. He walked into a bar and up to a man and said you owe me fifty bucks and the man stuck a knife in him.

The studio got to paint it in the papers. Life snuffed out, in a better place now. Other, bigger people died that day and needed column space. The short of what happened.

The long of what happened was the urchin walked into a bar, looked over to a corner booth, and in that corner booth a man sat wearing a T-shirt with the little urchin's face on it. His young face on a new T-shirt. The urchin might have been in a haze of barbiturates, but this was still an odd sight in those days. Then the guy who owed him money blocked the view. Then: the demand.

Then: the stab.

The urchin crawled the length of the bar to the corner booth and clutched on to the T-shirt, and the man wearing it had no idea who this dying awkward urchin was but the urchin held tight and his own young face filled the screen, accompanied him into death.

The man the urchin held on to in his final moments had seen some shit, and wasn't the type who thought much of staring down death. This wasn't a main moment of the man's week. The man didn't even think to wash the clothes right away.

THE LAW OF EXPANSION

BRIAN EVENSON

1.

Sabra, can you come up here?

—I'm busy.

—You're always busy. I wouldn't ask if I didn't need your help.

—Oh, all right . . . How did that happen?

—It doesn't matter.

—Is he dead?

—What do you think? Of course he's dead. See, it comes right off.

—Jimmy! Why would you show me that? What's wrong with you?

—Sorry . . . Here, you take the legs and I'll take the heavier half. We'll have to tuck his head into his shirt somehow. It'd be a lot easier if he was wearing a T-shirt, but at least this shirt is baggy. Between the two of us—

—We can't move him, Jimmy. We've got to leave him there.

—Why?

—Why? For the police. They have to come and take pictures and all that.

—The police? Oh, I don't think there's any point in bringing the police in on this, do you?

—Yes, of course I do. That's what the police are for.

—I think that would just complicate matters . . . Besides, they're already so busy . . .

— . . .

— . . .

—Well, we definitely have to tell Mom.

—We definitely *shouldn't* tell Mom.

—It's her boyfriend, Jimmy! It's Dale, for God's sake. She has a right to know.

—Was her boyfriend. Really, Sabra. You can't tell Mom.

— . . .

— . . .

—Goddamnit, this is just like Mr. Emmons all over again.

—I can't believe you'd say that! This is nothing

like what happened with Mr. Emmons! That was a complete accident!

—So you're saying this wasn't?

—Of course it was, but it was a completely different kind of accident . . .

—Hmm.

—We really should get him out of here and clean up.

—How did it happen, Jimmy?

—Oh, you know. These things happen.

—These things happen? Just what is that supposed to mean? I swear to God, Jimmy. I was right. This *is* just like Mr. Emmons all over again!

—It's not at all like Mr. Emmons!

—All right, then, prove it. How did it happen?

—I was just sleeping in bed, when suddenly I heard something. I sat bolt upright in bed and there he was, looming over me. I'm pretty sure he was planning to kill me. I hardly had time to think. I just lashed out.

—Why would he want to kill you?

—How do I know? I'm not in his head.

—And you just happened to have a knife on your bedside table . . .

—I'd . . . No, I think he must have had the knife. Probably he dropped it when I sat bolt upright.

—Stop saying bolt upright! This is not a novel! The police are going to think you're making it up!

—There's not a better way to say it! And we're not calling the police!

— . . .

—Anyway, probably he dropped the knife when I sat bol—when I sat suddenly up. My hand just happened to accidentally close over the handle when it fell. And then I lifted my arms to defend myself and accidentally killed him.

—Naturally.

—Naturally.

—By decapitating the poor man.

—He was a son of a bitch.

—Yes, he was, but that's no reason to decapitate him.

—I . . . don't know exactly how that happened. But you have to admit, he shouldn't have been in my room.

—What's Mom going to think?

—We're not going to tell Mom.

—I'm going to go tell Mom.

—Sabra?

—What?

—Last warning.

2.

—Kimmy?

—Yes?

—Is Mom still gone?

—Yes . . . Why? What's that on your shirt?

—Don't worry about that. Can you help me with something?

—It looks like blood. Is it blood?

—Don't freak out.

—Oh shit, Jimmy! Did something happen like happened with Mr. Emmons?

—Why does everybody fucking bring up Mr. Emmons? That wasn't my fault!

—What happened, Jimmy? What have you done?

—All right, look. I haven't done anything. Before I open this door, I want you to understand that. I came up here and found them like this.

—Them? There's two this time? What did you do to them?

—Nothing. I just finished explaining that. Focus, Kimmy. Take a deep breath. Now, look, you're my little sister, and I need your help and your understanding. Can you give me that?

—I'll . . . I'll try.

—Okay then. I'll show you.

— . . .

— . . .

— . . .

—Kimmy?

—Sabra, Jimmy? Sabra? I mean, I can understand Mr. Emmons. Or no, not really *understand*, but I can see how it might have happened for someone like you. But your own sister?

—I had nothing to do with it.

—And just who is the other one?

—That? Oh, that's Dale.

—Mom's boyfriend? How did you even recognize him?

—You see that big lump in the shirt? That's his head.

—How did his head end up not . . . attached to him?

—I don't know. It was like that when I got here.

—Jimmy, this is so much worse than Mr. Emmons.

—Kimmy, focus. I need you to focus. I didn't do this. I told you that already. Best I can figure it, Dale grabbed Sabra and dragged her into my room to rape then kill her, but Sabra fought back and fought back hard. She wrested his knife away from him.

—Wrested?

—Wrested. Am I not pronouncing it right?

—How should I know? It's not a word I've seen outside of detective novels. The police are never going to believe you if you—

—We're not calling the police!

—Okay, okay. Calm down.

—Here's how I reconstruct it. She *wrested* the knife away and then cut off his head, and then died herself.

— . . .

—Kimmy?

— . . .

—What do you think? Do you believe me when I say that's what happened?

—Of . . . course I believe you.

—Where are you going?

—Nowhere. I'm just going to . . . I forgot about something I was supposed to—

—Kimmy.

—Did you lock it? I didn't even see you lock it! Why would you want to lock us both in with those bodies? Mom? Mom!

—Mom's still gone, Kimmy.

—She'll be home any minute, Jimmy.

—Yes, that does pose a problem. We'll have to work fast.

— . . .

—I don't think you're listening to me, Kimmy. I don't think you're seeing yet what really happened. Kimmy, pay attention.

—Open the door! Jimmy, please, please!

—Oh, Kimmy. I'm very disappointed in you.

TRAIN DE NUIT

FABIEN CLOUETTE & QUENTIN LECLERC

Nous avons fui le terrain jonché de cadavres. À cause de nos expérimentations occultes, la ville était à feu et à sang. La nuit s'était posée sur les toits comme une épaisse couche de pétrole; des phares éclairaient notre course à travers les rideaux de pluie; nous entendions des cris qui étaient ceux d'hommes sans raison, mais qui ne pouvaient dissiper les dernières paroles de la désensorceleuse: IN THE HORROR. Dans ces trois mots résidait notre seule piste pour mettre fin au chaos environnant. Pour autant, leur sens demeurait obscur.

Une fois dans la gare, toujours en trombe, nous avons à peine jeté un œil sur le tableau d'affichage et

NIGHT TRAIN

FABIEN CLOUETTE & QUENTIN LECLERC

TRANSLATED BY JEFFREY ZUCKERMAN

e fled the corpse-strewn terrain. Our experiments in the occult had the town in fire and blood. Oil-thick night soaked into the roofs; headlight beams lit our way through surges of rain; frenzied screams reached our ears but could not erase the disenchantress's last words: IN THE HORROR. Those three words promised an end to the circumambient chaos. Their meaning, however, remained an enigma.

At the train station, we kept running and barely glanced at the departures board before hopping on the first train for Rennes. Dead pixels dotted the

nous sommes précipités dans le premier train en partance de Rennes. À l'intérieur des voitures, tous les panneaux LED semblaient détraqués, saturés de pixels morts. Parfois un prénom défilait, Edgar, qui nous était inconnu. Parfois, à côté de ce prénom, il y avait comme des dates de naissance et de décès (†). Nous avons traversé une dizaine de voitures, toutes absolument vides. Pas un contrôleur en vue. Les carreaux étaient embués et exhalaient une brume de condensation. La vue sur le paysage nocturne et pluvieux était totalement brouillée. Des gouttes venaient fouetter les vitres avant de courir ensuite à l'horizontale. Les annonces sonores avaient été remplacées par des interférences électriques et divers bips réguliers. Dans la pénombre de la dernière voiture où nous avons pénétré, cinq voyageurs étaient installés. Le néon halogène crépitait avec les à-coups du train. Ils semblaient discuter mais leur conversation nous était inaudible.

« Ils sont arrivés », déclara aussitôt un vieillard chauve avec un haut-de-forme et une moustache blanche. Ils se retournèrent alors tous au même instant et nous envisagèrent des pieds à la tête. « Ce sont eux qui sont censés résoudre l'enquête ?... » demanda une autre voyageuse d'une dizaine d'années, sceptique, assise à côté de sa jumelle. « Ceux de la dernière fois semblaient plus compétents. » En face d'elle se trouvait une très belle personne sans genre, habillée d'une robe rouge et d'un châle noir, et un VRP tenant fermement contre lui

LED screens in each car. Sometimes a name scrolled past, "Edgar": someone we didn't know. Sometimes, next to this name, a † as for birth and death dates appeared. The dozen cars we walked through were unremittingly empty. No ticket inspector in sight. The panes were cloudy and thick with condensation. Mist muddled every view of the sodden nighttime landscape. Raindrops hit the glass and joined all the others streaming along the metal housing. The intercom announcements had deteriorated to static and occasional beeps. In the murkiness of the final car, we found five passengers sitting. The lights overhead flickered with every jolt. They seemed to be talking, but their words were inaudible.

Then we heard them. "They're here," an old man with top hat and mustache said to the other four. They all turned in unison to appraise us. "They're the ones who'll fix this?" another passenger, sitting next to her ten-year-old twin, asked skeptically. "The last ones seemed smarter." Facing them were an androgynous beauty, wearing a red dress and a black wrap, and a sales rep clutching a locked briefcase beneath his name tag (JOHN-JOHN FLORANCE, COLLECTOR). "Pay them no heed!" the first man shouted. "Come, sit!"

The train jerked, then stopped. We noticed two strangers standing out by the tracks, half-hidden in the thickets, unmoving, staring at the machinery.

217

une mallette verrouillée et un badge à son nom (JOHN-JOHN FLORANCE, RECOUVREMENT). « Ne les écoutez pas, reprit le vieillard, je vous en prie, asseyez-vous ! »

À peine nous étions-nous assis que le train s'arrêta en pleine voie. Nous avons remarqué deux inconnus qui patientaient sur le bas-côté, à moitié dans les fourrés, immobiles, et qui fixaient la machine. Le vieil homme se leva, attrapa un micro dissimulé dans un coffrage du compartiment et annonça: « Pont sur le Vicoin, 5 minutes d'arrêt ! Veuillez descendre sur les voies et gagner les voitures de tête pour faciliter le passage du pont, merci ! » Nous sommes sortis du train et avons marché un moment au-dessus du cours d'eau, en compagnie des cinq voyageurs de notre voiture, rejoints bientôt par les deux inconnus du bas-côté. Nous avons traversé le pont, depuis le haut duquel le vieillard tenta de se jeter avant que nous ne le rattrapions in extremis. Les deux voyageurs, plutôt que de nous suivre à l'intérieur du train, sont restés sur le bas-côté. Le vieillard nous expliqua pourquoi il avait voulu sauter: « Pour me baigner, pardi ! »

À peine quelques minutes plus tard, le haut-parleur annonça l'arrêt suivant à Bif-de-la-Roche. Cette fois-ci, une cinquantaine d'inconnus nous observaient depuis le quai. Aucun ne monta à bord. Le train repartit. La personne à la robe rouge, Camille, se leva et se tourna vers le vieillard, à qui elle s'adressa presque en chantant en catalan: « Deux amoureux marchent sur le pont, un seul cadavre passe en dessous ! », avant de quitter le

The old man lumbered over to a microphone, and announced: "Bridge over the Vicoin, five-minute stop! Please exit directly onto the tracks and go to the cars up front, thank you very much!" We followed the five fellow passengers out to the river and the two strangers. As we crossed the bridge, the old man tried to jump off but we caught him in time. The strangers, rather than joining us aboard the front cars, stayed by the tracks. The old man was explaining why he wanted to jump: "To take a bath, by God!"

Moments later, the intercom announced the next stop: Bif-de-la-Roche. This time, fifty strangers were watching us from the platform. None came aboard. The train started again. The one in the red dress, Sorrel, stood and turned to the old man, practically singing in Catalan—"Two lovers walking over the bridge, one corpse passing by under!"—before walking through the doorway to drive the train. The lights crackled and strobed the murky compartment. The travelers' grimaces flared in the white flash before each new burst of black.

The twin girls simultaneously checked their watches every thirty seconds, each time insisting they'd be "late to see the game and meet the winners," then bursting into tears. When we ventured a question, one of the sisters aimed a Colt at us and shot five blanks while asking: "A five-bullet suicide, that's impossible, isn't it, Jimmy? So who pulled the

compartiment pour conduire le train. À peine eut-elle franchi la porte que les néons se mirent à grésiller et plongèrent la pièce dans une pénombre stroboscopique. Les voyageurs semblaient nous faire des grimaces dans les alternances de phases lumineuses et de phases obscures.

Les deux jumelles consultaient leurs montres toutes les trente secondes en parfaite synchronisation, et déclaraient à chaque fois qu'elles relevaient la tête qu'elles allaient être « en retard pour voir le match, pour parier sur l'équipe gagnante », avant de fondre en larmes. Quand on leur demanda où allait le train, l'une des sœurs braqua un colt (double canon) sur nous et tira cinq balles à blanc. « Un suicide à cinq balles, ça n'existe pas, n'est-ce pas Jimmy ? Alors, qui a tiré ? » nous demanda-t-elle. Le sixième coup partit dans la main du vieillard. « Dans la paume du vieillard, il y a un trou qui est comme un judas ! » déclara l'autre sœur. « Regarde dedans, c'est du passé. » Quelques éclairs aveuglants firent redoubler l'averse à l'extérieur, qui bientôt battit le toit de la machine comme une avalanche de coups de poing. Le flash lumineux fit apparaître pendant un instant le reflet du vieillard dans la vitre, mais ce reflet était celui d'un très jeune homme. Puis le tonnerre balaya le compartiment d'un noir assourdissant.

Soudain, troisième arrêt à Chartres. Deux-cents voyageurs immobiles sur le quai bondé. Cette fois-ci, ils se précipitèrent vers les entrées, mais le train demeurait

trigger?" The sixth shot went through the old man's hand. "His palm's got a hole like a peephole!" the other sister remarked. "Look, you can see the past." The storm outside redoubled, its blinding thunderbolts battering the metal in an endless fusillade. The fluorescent light briefly showed the old man's reflection in the glass as that of a young boy before thunder swept the compartment with a deafening darkness.

Then the third stop at Chartres. Two hundred transfixed travelers on the packed platform. This time they rushed toward the train, but it remained empty. The old man sidled over. "Jimmy Arrow once swore to shoot a film that would be the end of the world. Because he killed a man, you know." He looked through the bloody hole in his palm. "See for yourself, here's his face." Apart from the already festering wound, we saw nothing—if not a few vague shapes possibly reminiscent of a battlefield. But that was just his skin.

No announcement heralded the train's final stop. The old man and the twins packed up. Before we could do so, John-John Florance pulled us aside. "Here's the cassette," he whispered. His hand drew a VHS out of the briefcase. "There's other secrets in here, you know, but there's no possible price . . ." The sleeve bore the words *Jimmy Arrow—The Horror* above an illustration of frozen travelers, all looking at

vide. Le vieillard s'approcha de nous et regarda à travers sa paume trouée et ensanglantée. « Jimmy Arrow avait un jour dit qu'il tournerait un film qui serait la fin du monde », commença-t-il. « C'est parce qu'il a tué un homme vous savez. Regardez dans le trou de ma paume, il y a son visage ! » À part sa blessure qui commençait à s'infecter, nous ne voyions rien—sinon vaguement quelques formes qui pouvaient faire penser à un champ de bataille. Mais c'était juste la forme de la chair.

Aucune annonce sonore n'indiqua le terminus. Le train s'immobilisa subitement. Le vieillard et les deux jumelles rangèrent leurs affaires et s'apprêtèrent à sortir. Nous allions faire de même quand John-John Florance nous attira à l'écart. « Voici la cassette », nous dit-il tout en sortant discrètement une VHS de sa mallette. «Vous savez, j'ai d'autres secrets dans ma mallette, mais je ne peux pas vous les montrer, ils sont trop précieux!» chuchota-t-il comme un enfant. *Jimmy Arrow—The Horror*, était-il inscrit sur la jaquette. L'illustration représentait une foule de voyageurs immobiles, le regard fixe, perdus dans une brume opaque. Quand nous avons abaissé le boitier et regardé par les fenêtres du train, sur le quai, les mêmes milliers d'inconnus nous observaient. Nous ignorions tout de la gare dans laquelle nous étions arrivés.

one thing, lost in a nebulous fog. Our eyes shifted to the train windows, to the platform, to those selfsame strangers watching us. And nowhere could we see any name for the station.

WHAT WE KNOW

MISHA RAI

Red and blue police lights pierce the brushwood along the Grand Trunk Road, lighting up cutcha country roads and tunneled man-made cavities that house stolen cars and men like us. Whole towns have been emptied of illumination by the curfew imposed by Indira Gandhi's Emergency. Still, at night, our kind had been able to slip around in perpetual darkness. The death of the Galgotia couple, though, has made it hard for us to walk unseen from one part of town to another. We can hear their walkie-talkies through our scrounged-together police scanner. The deaths have bumped us up on the government radar, though this isn't the first double murder we've committed.

We know concussing people will eventually have consequences and are prepared for certain carnage.

We aren't the first of our kind who earn a livelihood by breaking into people's homes while stripped down to our underwear, slathered in oil, an iron-bound bamboo stave in our hand. Reasonable success of our predecessors rested on the idea that if homeowners woke up and tried to stop us, they found it hard to hold on to us. Their hands left grasping, smelling of something familiar. By the time they wrap their sleep-interrupted minds around what slipped through, sticks are tippy-tapped on their skulls, slipping them into unconsciousness.

Unlike the Oilies, the Slipperies, the Oiliests, the Slipperiests, the some-such gang ridiculously dubbed by the law, we need more than reasonable success. Most of us have been jobless since before the Emergency. The wrestling rings within which our frustrations met release closed down and there was no hope for amateur wrestlers or Kabbadi champions anymore.

Sola Singh, the first of our kind to legend, was caught because the housewife of a gold merchant held on to his handlebar moustache even after he head-butted her four times. The hair in her hand, along with fingerprints around her neck, created a file on him. Even though Nagendra Dhanda managed to run off, he left a trail of blood that led to him. Drona Gahlot was caught because of vanity. The ringworm-shaped birthmark on his right thigh had him leading robberies in long drawstring boxer shorts. On several occasions fabric from the shorts was found rippling on a doornail. Mika Singh was old and he couldn't run to safety, tripping on a root in the garden breaking his kneecap. Jyoti Chowdhary waited for his brother. Silva Singh's earring was torn out. Gogi Malik, his sacred thread. Nalli Singh broke his stick and stopped to collect the pieces.

The Mustard-Oil Loincloth Gang made changes. We retired older members, giving them a share of our earnings in grain and jaggery and milk. We looked for men in whom anger built slowly. We divided ourselves to hit different houses at the same time, breaking up fathers and sons, and brothers from brothers, and friends from friends. We broke into our closed wrestling haunts, playing Kabbadi to keep our bodies fit. We shaved ourselves from head to toe. We oiled our bodies thoroughly, including our buttocks. We used one type of scented oil for a month at a time. We exchanged regular underwear for white loincloths. We never let our women wash the loincloths. We used a concoction of bleach and phosphorus to keep them sparkling white. Every few months we burnt them deep in a farmer's field. We swaddled ourselves like babies fashioning the loincloths to resemble compact nappies. If anyone pulled off our loincloths we left them in their hands. We rid ourselves of all other items of dress.

We never carry the same stick twice.

On entering a home we first locate its occupants and give their skulls a single bash. If they wake up during our looting, they are often confused. Swimming vision can result in multiple numbers of shiny midair nappies walking around. Some of our victims are convinced of being haunted and lose use of their limbs and control of their bowels. Some mumble around in shock, giving us time to collect whatever we can and escape. Others who wake up with functioning mental faculties are treated with a harder blow. Sometimes, a fatal stroke.

The Galgotias fell into the latter category. Their house was a last-minute addition to our robbery route. This was to be our final bit of dacoity until the towns settled back to a stable rhythm. There were rumors of the Emergency ending and people were asking for accountability. So many arrested without clear cause and kept without trial. Faint murmurs had reached the army and police headquarters. There were rumors of new deployments to areas of unrest.

The Galgotias were known to have gold and diamonds stashed, hidden inside the sewing machines Mrs. Galgotia used. Their gardener, before he went north, told his card-playing brothers about the small godown at the back of the garden, full of packaged maize and potatoes and instant milk mixes. We knew where the key to its door hung. Both of them, husband and wife, needed more than one hard blow and instead

228

of going feeble from internal hemorrhaging there was brain splatter. Mr. Galgotia, a light sleeper, woke up to the sound of the kitchen window being smashed. He tried to load his father's old service gun but one of us pulped his skull in. Mrs. Galgotia's body was left half off the bed, her hair sticking thick with blood, her sari riding up her varicose-veined thighs. Shit and piss soaking it, running down her legs.

We didn't know at the time that their older daughter had disappeared three days ago and that Mr. Galgotia created a scene in front of the old constabulary. Since the start of the Emergency no one could get face time with any officer. And when the rumors began, they were all busy preparing to abandon their current postings. Mr. Galgotia went to ask for help anyway.

The duty constable first showed Mr. Galgotia the ledger for all the people who went missing at the start of the Emergency. He then opened another ledger with the names of the few people who had been found. After he closed both ledgers, he opened a book devoted to the conditions they were found in. We knew of this book. Inked in blue, at the end of each description were the initials of the police doctor. We were familiar with those descriptions. The duty constable tapped his index finger after each entry, leading Mr. Galgotia's eyes down that column. He then took out a missing persons form and placed it on the desk between them. We didn't fill out that form either. Mr. Galgotia spent

229

the rest of the day spitting on the outer walls of the constabulary until his wife dragged him home. When they were found on the evening after their murder everyone assumed it was the police who had paid them a visit.

The next morning the constabulary walls were embedded with hundreds of hoes.

Then today, mug shots of a white loincloth paper the town. We know now that a particular kind of unimagined buggery awaits us and hiding in our tunneled man-made holes is not going to be enough.

FINAL RESCUE

KENNETH NICHOLS

My clients come to me when the idea of their own mortality is a ghostly light on the horizon, a vague inevitability. They've arranged for life insurance, but their bodies and minds are still strong. Let's call this particular client Earle. His investment manager won't go the extra mile, won't feed the guard of his gated community a twenty-dollar bill and a story that I've always wanted to jog on the east side of Lake McGraw.

Maybe you stepped out on your husband or wife a couple decades ago and you couldn't bear to throw out the secret love letters that made your heart leap. I take care of it. No one will ever know you liked to cross-dress or what toys you hid under the bed. If anyone sees me tonight, they'll just guess I'm a new neighbor.

I have the kind of face people forget: an asset in my business.

We all have lines we won't cross. I won't hurt a child or a woman, and a man better truly deserve it. I won't destroy property without good reason. We all hold ourselves to standards but are happy to adjust them under the right circumstances. I'm still not sure that Earle did enough to convince me to cross the line.

I met Earle five years ago in the same manner as the rest of my clients. Talk turns serious in the clubhouse after the eighteenth hole, during the yearly sales convention, at the rivalry game alumni gathering. *You and yours are all set if something happens to you, right?* My client senses their friend is in need of something more. *I know a guy . . .*

In spite of the decades he had on me, Earle was in much better shape than I was. His handshake was that of a steelworker, not a Master of the Universe who made ungodly sums of money by moving numbers around on pieces of paper.

After some curt and guarded pleasantries, Earle told me he had a dog. "Bounder. A basset hound. My mother died last year. I was miserable for six months. Didn't leave the house. My business was suffering because I couldn't focus on anything. Then my son came home with this wrinkled lump of brown and white fur with floppy black ears that doesn't know how ridiculous it looks while running up to you on its stubby little legs. He found it at the dog pound, said it looked as lost as I was."

"You want me to ensure that the dog is cared for," I said. "A common request." I jotted "Dog—Bounder—Basset hound" into my notebook.

"Not quite," Earle said. "I want you to put him down."

I stopped taking notes. "Beg pardon?"

"Look, I'm healthy as a horse right now. My doctor says I'll outlive him. But every time I look into that goddamn dog's eyes, I can tell it loves me more than bacon. He's grateful I saved it from the gas chamber, gave it all my love. A couple weeks ago, I went on a business trip to Geneva; my housekeeper said that Bounder wouldn't budge from the corner of the yard."

I don't generally reveal personal information, but what I said seemed generic enough to share. "My mother had a Shar-Pei that followed her everywhere, like a duckling following its flock. When she died, that dog howled at the moon every night—something she had never done before. We knew she was calling for my mother. But we never thought of putting her down."

"I can afford your services because I have ideas that don't occur to other people. Will you show my dog mercy or not?"

I'm still not sure what I'll do at this moment, as I walk past Earle's stately pleasure dome. One of the rooms is lit; I imagine his widow is spending the early evening catching up on writing thank-you notes to those who sent flowers.

Earle wasn't lying; Bounder is a round lump of a dog. Earle was also prescient; Bounder is pressed into the corner of the chain-link fence thirty feet away from me, expecting Earle's car to arrive at any time. A security light detects my movement and flicks to life.

Basset hounds always look sad. This one was clearly in grief. The immutable equation: When does our grief outweigh potential joy? What do we do when we realize we can't be rescued again?

I take the chewy, bacon-flavored dog treat from my right coat pocket, the capsule from my left and press them together. The pill makes humans nauseated, makes them crawl to bed for a nap. The pill will make an old dog go to sleep and never wake up.

I fling the treat in one crisp, practiced motion. It lands five feet away from Bounder's powerful nose.

I never break my pace. I don't hear the rustle of those meaty, wrinkled legs moving his mouth to the food. I look back a couple times. Even with his face in shadow, I can see that Bounder is smart. He knows. He's not taking the bait.

Though I'm tempted to consider the job finished, I have another rule: I get confirmation whenever possible.

I return the next night, bribing the same guard the same twenty dollars for the same access to the jogging trail. What threat do I pose, a middle-aged guy in workout clothes?

Tonight, the house lights are out; I watched as

Earle's widow drove past the guardhouse. She doesn't need to be gone for long.

I'm not surprised to see Bounder pressed into his same corner. He knew I was coming. He knows what I'm doing. Still, I prepare his treat—two pills this time—and watch it thump to the grass beside him.

Bounder's head doesn't move. He stares at me, seeing more of the night than I do. Before I'm out of range, I look back and see Bounder still waiting, waiting for Earle to come home, to ruffle the folds of skin behind his floppy ears.

I return on the third night out of a sense of duty. This time, nearly every window of Earle's house is lit and a dozen cars line the long driveway. I see a number of figures in the windows; they're holding drinks and are clumped in small groups, likely trading sanitized stories about Earle and how flawless he was. Under normal circumstances, I might have called off the run, but that impulse dissipates when I see that Bounder is in the same place he was last night and the one before it.

Propelled by instinct, I keep my constant pace and fling the dog treat. It lands right in front of Bounder's snout.

Bounder slowly raises his chubby head and looks toward the house, where all of Earle's friends have gathered, no Earle to be found. He turns to look at the street Earle had used to come home to him thousands of times. Then he looks at me.

And eats the treat.

235

[PURPLE PILLS]

RION AMILCAR SCOTT

earest Slumlord,

    A cloudburst rained down upon me this morning, a shower of purple pills as I stood on my balcony. I opened my arms and twirled in the hard chemical shower.

Fuck! a voice from up in the clouds called out.

I took a pill in my hand. I twirled it between my fingers. I went inside to get a glass of water and I swallowed the purple salvation, letting it dance inside of me.

When I returned to the balcony, seven large black birds with long yellow beaks sat there snapping up my pills. They had eaten quite a few by this time. I yelled, cursed as the cloud had cursed. The birds fled, the cowards, and I contemplated taking another. Aren't pills always taken in pairs? I don't know. I took a second pill from the balcony floor and ushered it down my throat with a sip of water. I imagined a baby in a Moses basket drifting joyously on a rolling river. I took a third.

I went inside and sat. I peered ahead of me. The wall that always looked somewhat melted, it smoothed. I heard more cursing from above and it sounded less watery. Less like a wraithy-cloud, more like a woman. Yes, it was a woman.

I touched my face. The spinning world, always so slightly tilted found its kilter.

I took a deep breath and could no longer see the faces in the wind that always ambushed me and entered my nose whenever a strong breeze blew.

I could never even scarcely afford such sanity. And to have it rain down upon me . . .

A knocking sounded at my door. The bell trilled. When I pulled the door open, a wraith with long black hair—threaded with stray strands of silver—smiled upon me.

You must be the cloud, I said.

I dropped some blue pills, she replied. Panofil. I really, really need them back. I'm really sorry to bother you.

I pointed to the balcony and the cloud-woman passed through my living room. I said, But they're purple, my dear. She picked up the purple dots one by one and plinked them into an amber container.

Hey, she said. I dropped about twenty. There are only three here.

The birds, I said.

Fuck. Joker and Ernst are going to— Look, I'm sorry to disrupt you.

And the cloud was gone.

And I was here, for another several hours, I was here.

○

I strode to the balcony the next day hoping for another hard chemical shower. Thoughts were already piling up again in my head. More thoughts than the entire capacity of my skull. The faces in the wind had returned, and they brought with them their taunting. I knew now that I wasn't required to befriend them and this knowledge was like a good meal inside my stomach. It satisfied me, my love. Made me feel a warmth and a comfort, but it was also slowly turning to shit as I stood and I waited and I knew that after the satisfaction would come emptiness. And then, my slumlord, after falling empty I'd grow ravenous.

I stood in the autumn air. I opened my arms, and then I heard a voice from the sky. At first I thought it was one of the faces in the wind, but no it was the wraith, the cloud.

No, Kat, she said. No. They give me the pills on consignment. I have no clue how I'm going to make up the difference. She paused. Why the fuck do I even call y— You know what, Kat. I'll figure it out. She paused again. Why would you bring that up? I can't worry about shit down the fucking line right now. A pause. I am a felon, Kat. An F-E-L-O— Yes. I do blame you. My right thing and your right thing aren't the same, Kat. You know how much this shit costs at the pharmacy? So, yes, I am doing something good with my life. I'm like Robin Hood and you're standing in your fucking condo passing judgment. A pause, shorter than the rest. Are you going to help me out or not? Uh-huh. Fuck you, Kat. You owe me. Who said I should turn myself in and tell on Chappy, huh? That's how I got he— Hello? Hello? Fuck.

Just then I heard the wraith's feet thud above me, stomping inside her apartment. One of the birds from the previous day, one of the bastards who stole my pills from me, flew by singing a taunting song. I needed birdseed to dust my balcony floor with in order to lure back those thieving birds. I'd catch them and then use their long beaks to split open their stomachs to remove the purple pills in order to silence the faces of the winds.

O

You know that man who was murdered here months before me and my family moved in? Would you believe me when I tell you I see him late at night? That we shoot the breeze and sometimes he writes me letters? It's true, my slumlove. His pistol is here, stashed behind the water heater. He told me about it in one of his letters, an email. Initially, I planned to use the ghost gun to pick off those feathered fuckers one by one when they came to chomp on my birdseed, but when I went out to buy the seed I noticed the wraith's door was cracked and I figured, well, shit, I got this pistol. Stealing from the cloud-woman would be easier than stealing from the birds.

After I got my gun, I eased up the staircase, holding the silver pistol in front of me like they do in movies. I pushed the door slowly and stepped softly into the apartment. The place was a holy horror. The chairs and tables flipped, clothes and books and DVDs strewn about, porcelain lamps smashed to jagged shards against the floor. So much broken and torn down. No sign of the wraith living or dead. And who could have done this? Joker? Chappy? Ernst? Who knows? All I know is that whomever it was neglected to look behind the whistling water heater—that's where ghosts keep their pistols and cloud-wraith-women keep their drugs. And the cloud, the wraith? I don't know. I don't care, I suppose. I just want to be halfway sane for you, baby. This is why I eat these purple things now by the handful. Though I did some asking about the wraith. I heard a lot of things, some are harsh so I won't repeat them for your beautiful ears. What I choose to believe though is that the cloud-woman is safe, just on the run, in the wind like the faces who no longer bother me.

Sincerely and as always,

WE ARE SUICIDE

BENJAMIN PERCY

I work for the new mall. I'm the guy they hired to guard the spot where people keep killing themselves.

The mall doesn't look like much from the outside. But on the inside it's pretty nice. Fountains bottomed with sparkling quarters. A movie theater with reclining leather seats. Restaurants that serve twenty different types of hamburgers.

You don't expect bad things to happen in a place like this.

It started with a high schooler. She threw herself off the six-story parking structure. The square of concrete she hit is still stained a rusty brown. Like a mildewed gravestone that fell on its side.

Her friends and family made a memorial of flowers and teddy bears. They held a candlelight vigil. Somebody played the guitar and sang a song, but before he could finish it, a seventy-year-old woman dropped out of the sky and slammed the sidewalk. They say people twenty feet away got sprayed with her blood.

The mall closed the top level of the parking structure. But that didn't stop the man—Kinko's manager, divorced with two kids—from parking his car and leaving the door open and situating himself directly over that same stained slab of concrete.

With a pistol he ejected his brains out the back of his head.

That's why I'm here. Eight hours a day, I patrol the parking structure and the sidewalk below. The memorial continues to grow. The mall asked maintenance to clean it up, but more flowers and teddy bears kept appearing, so eventually they gave up. Petals snow across the concrete when the wind rises.

If I see someone lingering, maybe knuckling a tear from their eye, I ask, "How are you today?"

They will startle at the sound of my voice. Their lips will tremble when they say, "Fine," at a whisper and hurry away.

Except for this one lady. The lady in red. She works as a waitress at one of the restaurants that serves twenty different types of hamburgers. Her uniform is red pants and a red apron and a white-collared shirt.

I've noticed her more than a few times, jogging from the bus stop, late for her shift. Or taking a quick smoke break near the dumpsters out back.

"How are you today?" I ask her, and she doesn't say a word. Just looks at me with her eyes half-lidded, like she was on her way to falling asleep.

People not saying anything make me nervous. So I stupidly fill up the silence. "Feel that bite in the air?" I say. "Not too long until we'll be fighting the snow."

It is then that she reaches for the bulge inside her jacket.

I stutter-step toward her, my hands out—my mouth ready to shout no—but it's not a gun in her hand. It's a teddy bear. Slick red fur, white shirt with a hamburger emblazoned on it. She adds it gently to the memorial, one of thirty.

"Did you know her?" I ask.

Her voice is a rasp. "Which her?"

"Either her?"

"No. Not him neither." She gives me that sleepy stare again, shrugs. "Just felt like saying hello."

Before she heads toward the mall, she toes the stained square of concrete, like someone testing the water before diving in.

245

○

It's not like I'm a cop kicking down doors and shooting up warehouses. I'm not even an unshaven private investigator sucking on a flask and chasing down clues.

But eight hours a day, I walk the perimeter of a crime scene. That does something to you. Makes you think about what went wrong.

Some claim it's because of the election. The country is going to hell, as they see it, so they might as well too.

Others say it's contagious. "Endemic" is the word in the newspapers. Like a yawn. All I have to do is say that word—"yawn"—and you're already stifling one with your fist. Suicide apparently works the same way. You can catch it.

And still others say this place is haunted. Not the mall, but the soil it stands on . . .

This is Cliffs, Minnesota. We're a suburb of the Twin Cities now, but before that we were a town, and before that we were farms, and before that we were prairie and trees, and around that time we were the place where the army rounded up a bunch of Dakotas and hung them from trees like ornaments.

Maybe that's the reason. Maybe the stain is bigger

than I can see. Maybe there's something soaked into the very spirit of this place.

I didn't see it happen. I was patrolling the parking garage.

I found a huddle of people gathered on the sidewalk. A woman in a black pantsuit spoke loudly into her cell phone, saying, "Just send somebody!" Someone let out a whimpering mewl.

I rushed over and pushed through their bodies and the lady in the pantsuit said, "Oh, thank God," as if I could somehow make a difference.

The lady in red lay on the sidewalk, sprawled across the stained square of concrete. She hadn't jumped. She hadn't shot herself. Her eyes remained half-lidded even in death. I tried to close them but they sprung back.

The red of her apron might as well have been blood.

Why the mall?

People are supposed to come here to eat giant pretzels smeared with mustard and get their hair styled and try on sunglasses and sit in the massage chairs. This is supposed to be a place where every kind of person comes together and forgets about their shitty problems.

Maybe that's not possible anymore. And maybe the mall just feels like one big million-pound reminder that that's not possible anymore. A concrete sarcophagus.

But what do I know? I can't even do my job.

Four o'clock is sundown. The sodium lamps throw cones of light I hurry between. Something that is not quite snow sparkles in the wind. I keep hearing noises—like a whimper or the scud of a shoe—that make me spin around.

I feel safest near the memorial.

Some grit patters my shoulder and I look up. I'm not sure what I see—on the top level of the parking garage—but I see something. Black and ragged as a crow's wings. I do not say, "How are you today?" I say, "Stop!"

By the time I get up the staircase, my lungs are heaving and my pulse throbs in my ears.

I buckle on a pistol every morning. This doesn't seem strange to me until now. I'm supposed to be the guy who prevents death, not causes it.

I see nothing, no one. But the gun remains in my hand. It feels as right there as a finger.

Why did I take the job? Because it paid thirteen dollars an hour and seemed like an easy gig. But then it started to get to me. Gnaw at me. The stuffed animals and the flowers and the stain, the stain, the stain, soaking into me.

I creep across the empty stretch of concrete—until I reach the edge. I have become the dark shape. Up here the wind is hard enough and cold enough that my vision blurs, so that I think I can see all of them waiting for me down there, their arms wide open and waiting to catch me when I fall.

ALIBI

CHARLES YU

What do I have to say for myself? Okay. Fine. I was there. Yeah, I realize that's not a good alibi. I was there at the scene of the crime, at the time the crime occurred. Terrible fact pattern for me, I admit. Worst possible alibi. Kind of the opposite of an alibi. Like, as in, I don't really have an alibi. But you know I didn't do anything wrong. How do you know that? Well, for starters, I'm a good person. Good people don't do things like what's being alleged. How do I know I'm a good person? Because, I don't hurt people. You can look it up. My track record: I don't hurt people. Intentionally. Except for those closest to me. But everyone does that. That's just called human nature. We hurt our loved ones. So yeah, I hurt them, sometimes. I don't hurt strangers. Unless they cut me off. Or change lanes without signaling. Or look like they're about to. I've flipped a bird or two in my time. May have spanked a kid in anger. My kid, I mean. Obviously I would never spank anyone else's kid. Although I can think of a few who've probably deserved it. But I restrain myself. Because: that's the kind of person I am. Restrained. Non-spanking, mostly. Maybe I judge people, but who doesn't? Who doesn't enjoy doing that, in the privacy of his own home, own head? That doesn't make me a monster. Or a criminal. It makes me pretty normal, I think. Shows I have a conscience. I have morals and standards. Ask my spouse, my neighbors, my co-workers. They'll all tell you. Good dude, decent dude. I don't cheat on my taxes. Not any more than anyone else does. So what do I have to say for myself? I'll tell you what: I don't appreciate this line of questioning. Being interrogated, like I'm guilty of something. Especially when we all know who the real problem is. Not me. It's them. It's him. You know it is. I'm one of the good guys. You even said it: I was a witness. So why do I feel like now I'm a suspect? Of course I'm being defensive. You try sitting here, getting interrogated for just keeping to yourself, for living your life, going along, not hurting anyone, staying out of everyone's way. See how you like it. You know I didn't do anything wrong. Maybe I didn't do anything right, either. Maybe I watched it go down. Still watching it now. As the crime is ongoing. As the crime is turning out not to be at all what I thought was being alleged. Is being a bystander a crime now? If so, then fine. You got me. I'm guilty of being a bystander. If that's a crime then I'm guilty. All this, going on around me, but I did absolutely nothing. Guilty as charged. I'm guilty. I'm guilty. I'm guilty. I am.

PERMISSIONS ACKNOWLEDGMENTS

"See Agent." Copyright © 2018. Printed by permission of the author.

"Good Hair." Copyright © 2018 by Marta Balcewicz. Printed by permission of the author.

"Minor Witchcraft." Copyright © 2018 by Chiara Barzini. Printed by permission of the author.

"The Hall at the End of the Hall." Copyright © 2018 by Ryan Bloom. Printed by permission of the author.

"Night Train." Copyright © 2018 by Fabien Clouette and Quentin Leclerc, translated by Jeffrey Zuckerman. Printed by permission of the authors. The preceding portion of this novel-in-installments was published in *The White Review*'s June 2017 issue.

"A Bead to String." Copyright © 2018 by Michael Harris Cohen. Printed by permission of the author.

"Knife Fight." Copyright © 2018 by Julia Elliott. All rights reserved. Printed by permission of the author.

"Nobody's Gonna Sleep Here, Honey" first appeared in *BuzzFeed*. Copyright © 2018 by Danielle Evans. Reprinted by permission of the author.

"The Law of Expansion." Copyright © 2018 by Brian Evenson. Printed by permission of the author.

"nobody checks their voicemails anymore not even detectives." Copyright © 2018 by Sasha Fletcher. Printed by permission of the author.

"The Odds." Copyright © 2018 by Amelia Gray. Printed by permission of the author.

"Ghost Light." Copyright © 2018 by Elizabeth Hand. Printed by permission of the author.

"Exit Interview." Copyright © 2018 by Christian Hayden. Printed by permission of the author.

"The Luser," by Yuri Herrera, translated by Lisa Dillman. Copyright © 2018. Printed by permission of the author.

PERMISSIONS ACKNOWLEDGMENTS

"Give Me Strength." Copyright © 2018 by Karen Heuler. Printed by permission of the author.

"Airport Paperback." Copyright © 2018 by Adam Hirsch. Printed by permission of the author.

"Actual Urchin." Copyright © 2018 by Henry Hoke. Printed by permission of the author.

"Any Other." Copyright © 2018 by Jac Jemc. Printed by permission of the author.

"Ratface." Copyright © 2018 by Paul La Farge. Printed by permission of the author.

"Circuit City" first appeared in *The Arkansas International*. Copyright © 2018 by J. Robert Lennon. Reprinted by permission of the author.

"Mary When You Follow Her." Copyright © 2018 by Carmen Maria Machado. Printed by permission of the author.

"Three Scores." Copyright © 2018 by Nick Mamatas. Printed by permission of the author.

"The Trashman Cometh." Copyright © 2018 by J. W. McCormack. Printed by permission of the author.

"The Meme Farm." Copyright © 2018 by Adam McCulloch. Printed by permission of the author.

"No Exit." Copyright © 2018 by Fuminori Nakamura, translated by Allison Markin Powell. Printed by permission of the author.

"Withhold the Dawn." Copyright © 2018 by Richie Narvaez. Printed by permission of the author.

"Final Rescue." Copyright © 2018 by Kenneth Nichols. Printed by permission of the author.

"Hygge" first appeared in *Harper's Magazine*. Copyright © 2016 by Dorthe Nors. English translation © by Misha Hoekstra. Reprinted by permission of the author.

"We Are Suicide." Copyright © 2018 by Benjamin Percy. Printed by permission of the author.

"The Fifth of July." Copyright © 2018 by Helen Phillips. Printed by permission of the author.

PERMISSIONS ACKNOWLEDGMENTS

"What We Know." Copyright © 2018 by Misha Rai. Printed by permission of the author.

"[Purple Pills]." Copyright © 2018 by Rion Amilcar Scott. Printed by permission of the author.

"These Are Funny, Broken Days" was first published by *New York Tyrant*. Copyright © 2018 by Amber Sparks. Reprinted by permission of the author.

"Loophole." Copyright © 2018 by Adam Sternbergh. Printed by permission of the author.

"Friends." Copyright © 2018 by Laura van den Berg. Printed by permission of the author.

"The Rhetorician." Copyright © 2018 by Adrian Van Young. Printed by permission of the author.

"Dogface." Copyright © 2018 by Sarah Wang. Printed by permission of the author.

"Highway One." Copyright © 2018 by Benjamin Whitmer. Printed by permission of the author.

"The Wrong One." Copyright © 2018 by Erica Wright. Printed by permission of the author.

"Alibi." Copyright © 2018 by Charles Yu. Printed by permission of the author.

ABOUT THE EDITORS

LINCOLN MICHEL is the author of *Upright Beasts*, a collection of short stories from Coffee House Press. His fiction and criticism appear in *The New York Times*, *GQ*, *Granta*, *The Guardian*, *Rolling Stone*, the Pushcart Prize anthology, and elsewhere. With Nadxieli Nieto, he is the coeditor of *Gigantic Worlds*, an anthology of science flash fiction. He is a founding editor of *Gigantic* and the former editor in chief of *Electric Literature*. You can find him online at lincolnmichel.com.

NADXIELI NIETO is an editor and art director. She is the coeditor of *Carteles Contra Una Guerra*, which won the Premis Ciutat de Barcelona, and *Gigantic Worlds*, with Lincoln Michel. Formerly, she was the managing editor of the award-winning *NOON* annual and editor in chief of *Salt Hill* journal. Her poetry has appeared in publications such as *The New York Tyrant*, *West Wind Review*, and *Washington Square Review*, among others. She is on the steering committee of Latinx in Publishing (LxP). Her collaborative artist books may be found in the permanent collections of the Museum of Modern Art and the Brooklyn Museum.

ABOUT THE CONTRIBUTORS

WESLEY ALLSBROOK was born in Durham, North Carolina. She attended the Rhode Island School of Design. Then she moved to Brooklyn, New York. She has been recognized by the Art Directors Club, the Society of Publication Designers, the Society of Illustrators, American Illustration, Communication Arts, and the 3x3 Annual. She currently lives and works in Los Angeles, California. She draws for print, for the web, for comics, and for VR.

ANONYMOUS prefers to remain anonymous.

MARTA BALCEWICZ lives in Toronto. Her prose, poetry, and comics appear in *The Offing*, *Catapult*, *Hobart*, *Pithead Chapel*, *The Normal School*, and elsewhere.

CHIARA BARZINI is an Italian screen and fiction writer. She has lived and studied in the United States where she collaborated with Italian *Vanity Fair*, *GQ*, *XL Repubblica*, *Rolling Stone Italy*, *Flair*, and *Marie Claire* while publishing essays in American magazines such as *The Village Voice*, *Harper's*, *Vogue*, *Interview Magazine*, *Vice*, and *Rolling Stone*. Her fiction has appeared in *BOMB Magazine*, *The Coffin Factory*, *Noon*, *New York Tyrant*, *Vice*, and *Dazed & Confused*. She is the author of the story collection *Sister Stop Breathing* (Calamari Press, 2012) and *Things That Happened Before the Earthquake* (Doubleday, 2017). She has written a variety of screenplays for both television and film.

About the Contributors

RYAN BLOOM's work has appeared in *The New Yorker*, *Tin House*, *Guernica*, *New England Review*, *PEN America*, *Black Clock*, *The American Prospect*, and a variety of other publications. His translation of Albert Camus's *Notebooks 1951–1959* was nominated for the 2009 French-American Foundation and Florence Gould Foundation Prize for Superior English Translation of French Prose.

FABIEN CLOUETTE is the author of *Quelques Rides* (2015) and *Le Bal des Ardents* (2016), published by Éditions de l'Ogre. He is also a filmmaker and maritime anthropologist. He was born in 1989 in Saint-Malo.

MICHAEL HARRIS COHEN's work has been published or is forthcoming in various magazines and anthologies including *Fiction International*, *The Dark Magazine*, *Havok*, *Litro*, *Le Scat Noir*, and *Conjunctions* (web). He's the winner of the Weston Award from Brown University, Mixer's "Sex, Violence and Satire" contest and the Modern Grimmoire Literary Prize. He's a recipient of a Fulbright grant and fellowships from the Atlantic Center for the Arts, the Djerassi Foundation, the Jentel Artist's Residency, the Blue Mountain Center, and OMI International Arts Center for Writers. His first book, *The Eyes*, was published in 2013. He lives and teaches in Bulgaria.

LISA DILLMAN translates from the Spanish and teaches in the Department of Spanish and Portuguese at Emory University. Her translation of Yuri Herrera's *Signs Preceding the End of the World* won the 2016 Best Translated Book Award. She lives in Decatur, Georgia.

JULIA ELLIOTT's writing has appeared in *Tin House*, *The Georgia Review*, *Conjunctions*, *The New York Times*, and other publications. She has won a Rona Jaffe Writer's Award, and her stories have been anthologized in

Pushcart Prize: Best of the Small Presses and *Best American Short Stories*. Her debut story collection, *The Wilds*, was chosen by *Kirkus*, *BuzzFeed*, *Book Riot*, and *Electric Literature* as one of the Best Books of 2014 and was a *New York Times Book Review* Editors' Choice. Her first novel, *The New and Improved Romie Futch*, was published in October 2015.

DANIELLE EVANS is the author of the story collection *Before You Suffocate Your Own Fool Self*, winner of the PEN/Robert W. Bingham Prize, the Hurston-Wright award, the Paterson Prize, and a National Book Foundation 5 under 35 selection. Her stories have appeared in magazines and anthologies including *The Paris Review*, *A Public Space*, *American Short Fiction*, *Callaloo*, *New Stories from the South*, and *The Best American Short Stories*. She teaches creative writing at the University of Wisconsin–Madison.

BRIAN EVENSON is the author of a dozen books of fiction, most recently the story collection *A Collapse of Horses* (Coffee House Press) and the novella *The Warren* (Tor.com). He is the recipient of three O. Henry Prizes as well as an NEA fellowship. His work has been translated into French, Italian, Greek Spanish, Japanese, Persian, and Slovenian. He lives in Los Angeles and teaches in the Critical Studies Program at CalArts.

SASHA FLETCHER is the author of *it is going to be a good year* (Big Lucks Books, 2016). He lives in Brooklyn.

AMELIA GRAY is the author of five books, most recently *Isadora* (FSG). Her fiction and essays have appeared in *The New Yorker*, *The New York Times*, *The Wall Street Journal*, *Tin House*, and *Vice*. She is winner of the NYPL

About the Contributors

Young Lion, of FC2's Ronald Sukenick Innovative Fiction Prize, and a finalist for the PEN/Faulkner Award for Fiction. She lives in Los Angeles.

ELIZABETH HAND is the multiple-award-winning author of fifteen novels and five collections of short fiction, including the Cass Neary noir novels *Generation Loss*, *Available Dark*, and *Hard Light*, which have been compared to those of Patricia Highsmith. She is a longtime contributor to the *Los Angeles Times*, *The Washington Post*, *Salon*, and *The Village Voice*, among many others, and teaches at the Stonecoast MFA Program. Her forthcoming noir novel, *The Book of Lamps and Banners*, will be published in 2018. She lives on the Maine coast and in North London.

CHRISTIAN HAYDEN lives in Chicago, Illinois. His work has appeared in *[PANK]*, *Word Riot*, *Buffalo Almanack*, *Yemassee*, *McSweeney's Internet Tendency*, and others. He also contributes to *ClickHole*.

YURI HERRERA (Actopan, México, 1970). Has written three novels, all of them translated into several languages: *Signs Preceding the End of the World*, *Transmigration of Bodies*, *Kingdom Cons*, published in English by And Other Stories. He is currently an assistant professor at the University of Tulane, in New Orleans.

KAREN HEULER's stories have appeared in over one hundred literary and speculative magazines and anthologies, from *Conjunctions* to *Clarkesworld* to *Weird Tales*, as well as a number of Best Of anthologies. She has received an O. Henry award, been a finalist for the Iowa short fiction award, the Bellwether award, the Shirley Jackson award for short fiction (twice), and a bunch of other near-misses. She has published four novels and three story collections, and in July Aqueduct Press released her novella, *In Search of Lost Time*, about a woman who can steal time.

ADAM HIRSCH is a writer and filmmaker living in Los Angeles.

MISHA HOEKSTRA is an award-winning translator living in Aarhus, where he writes and performs songs under the name Minka Hoist.

HENRY HOKE is the author of *Genevieves* and *The Book of Endless Sleepovers*. He co-created and directs *Enter>text: a living literary journal*.

JAC JEMC is the author of *The Grip of It* (FSG Originals). Her first novel, *My Only Wife* (Dzanc Books) was a finalist for the 2013 PEN/Robert W. Bingham Prize for Debut Fiction and winner of the Paula Anderson Book Award, and her collection of stories, *A Different Bed Every Time* (Dzanc Books) was named one of Amazon's best story collections of 2014. She edits nonfiction for *Hobart*.

PAUL LA FARGE is the author of five books, most recently *The Night Ocean*, a novel. He lives in upstate New York, and whatever he's up to, he does his best not to get caught.

QUENTIN LECLERC is the author of *Saccage* (2016; Prix Littéraire des Grandes Écoles 2017) and *La Ville Fond* (2017), both published by Éditions de l'Ogre. He was born in 1991 and lives in Rennes.

J. ROBERT LENNON is the author of two story collections, *Pieces for the Left Hand* and *See You in Paradise*, and eight novels, including *Mailman*, *Familiar*, and *Broken River*. He teaches writing at Cornell University.

ABOUT THE CONTRIBUTORS

CARMEN MARIA MACHADO is the author of the story collection *Her Body and Other Parties* and the forthcoming memoir *House in Indiana*, both from Graywolf Press. She is a fiction writer, critic, and essayist whose work has appeared in *The New Yorker*, *Granta*, *Tin House*, *Guernica*, *Electric Literature*, *NPR*, *Gulf Coast*, *Vice*, and elsewhere. Her stories have been reprinted in *Best American Science Fiction & Fantasy* and *Best Horror of the Year*, and she holds an MFA from the Iowa Writers' Workshop. She is the Artist in Residence at the University of Pennsylvania, and lives in Philadelphia with her wife.

NICK MAMATAS is the author of several novels, including *The Last Weekend* and *I Am Providence*. His short fiction has appeared in *Best American Mystery Stories*, *West Coast Crime Wave*, *Long Island Noir*, *Vancouver Noir*, and many other venues.

J. W. McCORMACK's fiction and criticism have appeared in *Conjunctions*, *Tin House*, *Vice*, and *The Weird Fiction Review*. He lives in Brooklyn with his parakeet, Paul Atreides.

ADAM McCULLOCH is a NATJA award–winning travel writer whose work has appeared in *Travel + Leisure*, *The Australian*, *Men's Health*, *Reader's Digest*, *Lonely Planet*. His screenplays have been listed for the Academy Nicholl Fellowship in Screenwriting, Page International Screenwriting Awards, Scriptapalooza, and BlueCat Screenplay Competition.

FUMINORI NAKAMURA was born in 1977 and graduated from Fukushima University in 2000. His work has been translated into twelve languages, and he has won numerous prizes for his writing, including the Oe Prize, Japan's largest literary award; the David L. Goodis Award for Noir

Fiction; and the prestigious Akutagawa Prize. *The Thief*, his first novel to be translated into English, was a finalist for the Los Angeles Times Book Prize. His other novels include *The Gun*, *The Kingdom*, *Evil and the Mask*, *Last Winter, We Parted*, and *The Boy in the Earth*.

RICHIE NARVAEZ was born and raised in Williamsburg, Brooklyn. His work has been published in *Long Island Noir*, *Mississippi Review*, *Murdaland*, *Pilgrimage*, *Plots with Guns*, *Sunshine Noir*, and others. His first book of short stories, *Roachkiller and Other Stories*, received the Spinetingler Award for Best Anthology/Short Story Collection.

KENNETH NICHOLS earned his MFA in Creative Writing from Ohio State and maintains the writing craft website *Great Writers Steal* (www.great writerssteal.com). His work has appeared in a wide range of publications including *Main Street Rag*, *Literary Orphans*, and *Lunch Ticket*.

DORTHE NORS received the 2014 Per Olov Enquist Literary Prize for *Karate Chop*, which *Publishers Weekly* named one of the best books of 2014. Her work has appeared in *The New Yorker* and *A Public Space*.

BENJAMIN PERCY is the author of seven books, most recently *The Dark Net*, a novel. He writes the Green Arrow and Teen Titans series for DC Comics. His honors include an NEA Fellowship, the Whiting Award, the Plimpton Prize, two Pushcart Prizes, and inclusion in *Best American Stories*.

HELEN PHILLIPS is the author of four books, including, most recently, the short story collection *Some Possible Solutions*, winner of the 2017 John Gardner Fiction Book Award. Her novel *The Beautiful Bureaucrat*, a *New York*

ABOUT THE CONTRIBUTORS

Times Notable Book of 2015, was a finalist for the Los Angeles Times Book Prize and the New York Public Library's Young Lions Award. She is the recipient of a Rona Jaffe Foundation Writer's Award and the Italo Calvino Prize. Her work has appeared in *The Atlantic*, *The New York Times*, and *Tin House*, and on *Selected Shorts*. She teaches at Brooklyn College.

ALLISON MARKIN POWELL is a literary translator, editor, and publishing consultant. Her translation of Hiromi Kawakami's *The Briefcase* (U.K. title, *Strange Weather in Tokyo*) was nominated for the Man Asian Literary Prize and the Independent Foreign Fiction Prize. Her other translations include works by Osamu Dazai, Fuminori Nakamura, and Kanako Nishi. She lives in New York City, and maintains the database Japanese Literature in English.

On April 5, 2017, MISHA RAI was awarded the 2016 novel-in-progress award for *Blood We Did Not Spill* by the Dana Award in the novel category. In 2016 she became the first-ever PhD in Fiction to be awarded the Woodrow Wilson Dissertation Fellowship in Women's Studies for the same novel-in-progress. She has also been a 2016–2017 Edward H. and Mary C. Kingsbury Fellow at Florida State University and the recipient of the 2015 George M. Harper Award. Misha Rai was born in Sonepat, Haryana, and brought up in India. She currently serves as associate reviews editor for *Pleiades*.

RION AMILCAR SCOTT's short story collection, *Insurrections* (University Press of Kentucky, 2016) was awarded the 2017 PEN/Robert W. Bingham Prize for Debut Fiction. Presently, he teaches English at Bowie State University.

AMBER SPARKS is the author of the short story collection *The Unfinished World and Other Stories*, which has received praise from *The New York Times*, *The Washington Post*, and *The Paris Review*, among others. She is also the author of a previous short story collection, *May We Shed These Human Bodies*, as well as the co-author of a hybrid novella with Robert Kloss and illustrator Matt Kish, titled *The Desert Places*.

ADAM STERNBERGH is an Edgar-nominated novelist and *New York* magazine's culture editor, and the former culture editor of *The New York Times Magazine*. His latest novel is *The Blinds*, a thriller about a remote, secretive town in West Texas. His first novel, *Shovel Ready*, a future-noir thriller about a garbageman-turned-hitman in a dystopian New York City, was a *Newsweek* Favorite Book of 2014 and a 2015 Edgar Award nominee. Raised in Toronto, he lives in Brooklyn with his family.

LAURA VAN DEN BERG is the author of two story collections, most recently *The Isle of Youth*, and a novel, *Find Me*. Her next novel, *The Third Hotel*, is forthcoming from FSG in August 2018.

ADRIAN VAN YOUNG is the author of *The Man Who Noticed Everything*, a collection of stories, and *Shadows in Summerland*, a novel. His fiction and nonfiction have appeared in such publications as *The Collagist*, *Black Warrior Review*, *Conjunctions*, Electric Literature's Recommended Reading, *Slate*, *Vice*, *The Believer*, and *The New Yorker*. He lives in New Orleans, where he teaches at Tulane University.

269

SARAH WANG is a writer based in New York. In 2016 she was awarded a Chicago Tribune Nelson Algren Literary Award runner-up prize. She has written for *n+1*, *The Los Angeles Review of Books*, *Conjunctions*, *Stonecutter Journal*, *Joyland*, the Asian American Writer's Workshop, *Story Magazine*, *The Third Rail*, and *The Last Newspaper* at the New Museum of Contemporary Art, among other publications. An excerpt of her novel is forthcoming in *BOMB*. She is the co-editor of semiotext(e)'s *Animal Shelter*. See more of her work at wangsarah.com.

BENJAMIN WHITMER is the author of *Cry Father* and *Pike*, which was nominated for the 2013 Grand Prix de Littérature Policière, and co-author (with Charlie Louvin) of *Satan Is Real*, a New York Times Critics' Choice book. He lives in Colorado with his two children.

ERICA WRIGHT's latest novel is *The Granite Moth* (Pegasus Books), a sequel to *The Red Chameleon* (Pegasus Books). She is also the author of two poetry collections, *Instructions for Killing the Jackal* (Black Lawrence Press) and *All the Bayou Stories End with Drowned* (Black Lawrence Press). She is the poetry editor and a senior editor at *Guernica* as well as an editorial board member for Alice James Books.

CHARLES YU has published three books including his most recent, *Sorry Please Thank You*. His writing has been published in a number of publications including *The New Yorker*, *Wired*, *Slate*, and *The New York Times*. He has also written for shows on HBO and AMC.

JEFFREY ZUCKERMAN is the translator of Ananda Devi's *Eve Out of Her Ruins* (Firecracker Award in Fiction, 2017) and Jean-Jacques Schuhl's *Dusty Pink*, and is currently translating the complete stories of Hervé Guibert. He was born in St. Louis, Missouri, in 1987 and lives in New York, where he works as an editor for *Music & Literature* magazine.

INDEX

271

INDEX

272

273

INDEX

274